The Music Man

Book One of The Music Man series.

Written by Moonyani Write

DEDICATION

Thanks to everyone who helped me during this process.

For Carly
♡
Thank you!
6-2-23

Introduction

There was a man, a quiet man, who wouldn't speak. Every day,
he went into town, to buy groceries.
He would smile and nod, while tipping his hat. He walked briskly
and calmly, moving to a beat.
The leaves would crunch with the stomp of his feet. This man was
the Music Man.

Chapter 1

It was only 7 am in the small England town, you could hear
the wind snapping outside. The England town had cottages, with
buggies as transportation. The town also consisted of farms, with
a local butcher shop. The season was winter. There was snow
everywhere.

The Music Man was a simple man, living in a one-story house.
One bedroom, one bathroom, and a sitting room. He was content,
no one to bother
his space.
He had no family, no one to invite to his place. Then, a surprise
happened to arise.
A knock came from the door,
The Music Man looked in the peep hole and
Lo and behold,
There, stood a young boy, standing in the cold.

Chapter 2

The Music Man opened the door.

"May I help you?" he asked in his very mellow and inviting tone.

One could hear the wind whistling, the boy shivering.

"Yes, I am lost," the boy responded.

He had very light brown skin with deep dimples. His eyes were a darker brown and he wore a coat with worn slacks and snow boots.

"Whereabouts is your home?" the Music Man asked.

The Music Man was a tall, Black man. He had a very welcoming look about him, as his face was really gentle. His skin was smooth and dark, and his teeth were as white as pearls.

The boy replied, "Over the bridge, may I come in?" "It's freezing, bloody cold."

The Music Man hesitated and then sighed deeply. "Yes, you may come in."

"Would you like some tea?"

"Yes," the boy said as he sat on the sofa.

The Music Man reached into the pantry, grabbed a cup, and poured some tea. "Would you like some lemon with your tea?" he asked.

"No sir," the boy replied.

The Music Man said, "Hmm", with a sneer.

He picked the cup up slowly, walked to the boy, handed it to him, and then sat in his chair.

"May I have your name?" the Music Man asked.

"My name's Jimmy," the boy muttered after taking a sip of the warm tea. "Jimmy Jakes."

The Music Man replied, "Ah, why are you out in the cold?"

"Mum's harsh, and dad is gone," Jimmy replied.

"So, I ran away."

The Music Man replied, "Well, you must go back, she's probably worried sick."

"No sir, she hates me. She says she regrets my birth sir, every day."

"My dad left us penniless."

"Mom has to work every day in the cannery."

"So what is your plan?" the Music Man asked.

"I don't know, was going to make my way to London."

"Perhaps find work in the factory."

The young boy was no more than 13 years old.

"I like music though, it makes me happy."

"I think of melodies in my head."

"Well that's peculiar!" the Music Man shouted.

"So do I!" he added.

"What kind of melodies?" he also asked.

"Well, melodies that bring peace; waltzing, classical, anything beautiful," replied Jimmy.

"All music is beautiful, from waltzing to symphonies, it's all beauty," replied the Music Man.
Jimmy nodded, gripped his cup, and then wiped his eye. He was still shivering and rubbing his arms.
"Are you still cold?" the Music Man asked.

You could hear the wood burning in the fireplace, as it crackled and snapped. It smelled of burning oak, a home of serenity.
"Just a tad, may I have some more tea please?" Jimmy asked, as he extended his empty teacup, hardly still.
His lips were no longer dry and frost bitten.

The Music Man replied, "Yes, I will also fetch you a blanket and some long johns."
 "They were my boy's."
A sad look appeared in the Music Man's eyes.
He took a quick glimpse at Jimmy, his eyes started to water.
"He would've been around your age now."
"You resemble him."

Jimmy gulped and couldn't muster up the courage to ask what happened to him.

He made a promise to himself to save that discussion for a later time if there was one.

The Music Man then suddenly said, "He died in town."

"Wife was walking with him and they were ran over by a buggy."
 Jimmy looked down with sad eyes and replied, "I am sorry sir."

"It's alright," the Music Man replied.
"By the way, you can stay as long as you want."
"Now, how about some tea and a warm blanket?"
"You're still pale my boy."
"Yes sir, thank you," smiled Jimmy.

Chapter 3

Although Jimmy and his mother's relationship was not well, he had a puppy to keep him company. The puppy's name was Sebastian and he was a baby Shih Tzu. However, the days were short lived of their relationship. Jimmy took him to the beach quite frequently, running and playing with him. Sadly, one day, it was windy. Jimmy and Sebastian were playing catch in the sand. The weather wasn't too cold, as the snow was also partially melted. A little girl next to them was flying a kite with her father. His dog was excited at the kite and ran towards the sea. Jimmy ran really fast after him, screaming his name.
"Sebastian!" "Sebastian!"
In an instant, Jimmy's dog was swept away by the waves.

That was the closest friend he ever had. Jimmy sat down in the sand and cried, wiping the tears away.
The little girl, who witnessed the scene, went up to Jimmy, and sat beside him.
"Stephanie!" shouted the little girl's father.
"I'm sorry," said the little girl.

Jimmy looked up and wiped a tear from his eye.
 "What was his name?" she asked.
    "Sebastian," sobbed Jimmy.
   The little girl wrapped her arm on his shoulder.
   "Don't be sad."
   "He's in doggy heaven now."

Jimmy looked back up at the little girl. The little girl's father walked
up to them.
"I'm sorry about your dog," her father said.
"I know it's cold but,"
"Would you like some ice cream son?"
"No thanks," sniffled Jimmy.
"I should get going."

Jimmy got up, wiped the sand off his pants, and began walking
home.
He looked back and noticed the little girl staring at the ocean
waves.
He then started to cry again and ran home.

  "You didn't do the rest of your chores today son," said Jimmy's
mother as she was serving their dinner.
Jimmy sat in silence, with a blank look on his face.
"Where's Sebastian?" she asked, as she placed plates on the
table.
Jimmy looked up from the table and answered,

"He's gone."
"Was swept away at the beach."

"Oh no, " said his mother.

"I'm sorry Jimmy."
"Sigh."
"Dogs are messy anyway."

Jimmy looked furiously at his mother, in disbelief that she could've said such a thing.
He got up from the table, went to his room, and slammed the door.
The next morning, he ran away.

Chapter 4

As Jimmy slept on the couch for his nap, the Music Man gazed at him. The memories of his little boy and wife resurfaced and he started weeping. He remembered the last time he kissed his boy and wife, not knowing that would be the last. The Music Man then thanked God for Jimmy's presence, because now he had someone else to care for and maybe form a special bond with for the time being.
Jimmy woke up and sat up on the couch and yawned loudly.
 "You're up my boy," said the Music Man.
"Want some breakfast?"
 "Yes sir," Jimmy yawned.
The Music Man made his way to the kitchen.
He loved cooking.
Scrambled eggs, and bacon with toast were his favorite.

Jimmy smelled the aroma of the food and hurried to the kitchen table. "Slow down son," laughed the Music Man.

"Sorry sir, I haven't eaten in days," Jimmy said, as he stuffed his mouth.

"This is delicious!"

"I'm glad to hear that," the Music Man laughed again.

"Would you like to visit the attic?" he inquired.

"I have a piano up there."

"Really sir?" asked Jimmy, as his eyes widened.

"Mom taught me how to play when I was younger, but it's been a long time," he added.

"Well let's just see if it still works, it'll be an adventure," said the Music Man. Jimmy put his fork down and followed the Music Man. They walked up to the attic and there was dust everywhere. They both coughed, as the Music Man hadn't cleaned his attic in years.

"Oh wow!" Jimmy shouted, as he stared at the piano.

"It's huge! But how will we carry it downstairs sir?" he asked.

The Music Man put his finger next to his lips and was deep in thought. "Well, it got up here, so surely we can bring it back down."

He saw a cloth across the room, picked it up, and started cleaning the piano.

"We must clean it first so that we don't choke from the dust," the Music Man said.

"There's another cloth," he added.
"I'll help you," said Jimmy.
They both started cleaning the piano and the dust vanished.
"Now, time for the hard part," said the Music Man.

He walked over to the piano, kneeled down in front of it, and lifted one side. Jimmy then lifted the other side although he struggled.

"Hmmm, just concentrate and believe that you can lift it. And once we get it down there, you'll be able to play it," the Music Man said. They struggled to lift the piano, as Jimmy was just a young boy who did not use his muscles on a regular basis. Sure, he helped his mother move some things around their house, but a piano was certainly not one of those things. As for the Music Man, he walked daily, so he was in good shape. He was in his late thirties but needed someone to match his strength.
"We'll just have to ask my neighbors to help," the Music Man sighed.
"Their names are Michael and Morris."
"Friendly folks."

"They're a little older than you, perhaps in their younger twenties."
"I think with the four of us, we can manage."
"Want me to go ask them?" asked Jimmy in an excited manner.
"We'll go together," laughed the Music Man.
"Their mom usually has leftover cake every day."
"She's a baker in the city I believe."
"Anyway, they're very delicious."

"Come on, let's put on some decent clothes."

Jimmy followed the Music Man down the attic stairs in a hurried manner. "May I ask you a question sir?"

"Depends on the question," laughed the Music Man.
"Well, do you ever get lonely?"
"Living here by yourself?"

"I used to, when they died," the Music Man responded.
"But I have my music to write, that keeps me busy."
"I also go into the city about three times a week."
"Do you let anyone see your work sir?" asked Jimmy.
"Not yet," the Music Man replied.
"Not the right time."

"What are they about?" Jimmy also asked.

"Now now, when we get the piano down here, we can play them together."
"How does that sound?" the Music Man asked, with a smile.
"I can't wait!" shouted Jimmy.
"I know," the Music Man smiled.

The Music Man and Jimmy made their way to the nearby house. The house was very pretty, with clothes hanging on the line.
The Music Man knocked on the door, waiting for a response.

"Who is it?!" shouted a hoarse voice.
"It's Cornelius," said the Music Man in a confident manner.

The door swung open, and a tall, heavyset man stood there, towering them. He stood about six feet tall, with a sausage link in his hand.
"Mom's going to be so happy to see you," the man said, as he smacked his food.

"Mother!"

"Don't believe we've met?" asked the man, as he looked at Jimmy.
"Jimmy, this is Morris."
"Morris, this is Jimmy," said the Music Man, as he introduced them.
"Why, you're a handsome young man!" Morris shouted.
"Cornelius adopted you?" he also asked.

Jimmy wasn't sure what to say, and suddenly Morris's sausage was yanked out of his hand.
"Hey! That's mine!" shouted Morris.

His brother was much shorter than him and much thinner.

"Mom said you need to ease up on them, I will help you eat it!" the young man laughed.
"Jimmy, this is Michael."

"Michael, Jimmy," the Music Man said.

"Heck, do you want this sausage?" Michael asked Jimmy.

Jimmy chuckled, as he was taken aback at how well they got along.
 Jimmy then looked at the Music Man, unsure of what to say.
"We were just hoping that you could help us move the piano that's in the attic," said the Music Man.
"Of course these rascals can," a soft tone had spoken.

Michael and Morris's mother was a very short woman with short black hair and very pretty dark skin. Her eyes were brown and she wore glasses. Also, she was very thin.
"Cornelius, who is this handsome young man?" she asked.
 "Jimmy this is Ms. Lois."
"Ms. Lois, this is Jimmy," the Music Man said.
"She's Michael's and Morris's mother."
"Are you all hungry?" asked Ms. Lois.

"You shouldn't be lifting things on an empty stomach."
"We just ate breakfast actually."
"But cake afterward would be just fine," smiled the Music Man.
"Ahhhh, of course!" laughed Ms. Lois.

"I have a few leftovers for you all, yes yes."

Michael and Morris then made their way out of the house and shut the front door. "So, Cornelius is going to share his music with you eh?" asked Michael.
"I hope so," said Jimmy.

"You like music too?" asked Morris.
"Yes, I love it," Jimmy answered.
"Well you and Cornelius definitely have THAT in common," Morris smiled.

The four young men made their way to the attic to move the piano.
"Ah-choo!" sneezed Morris.
"Ouch!"

Morris hit his head against the ceiling as he entered the attic.

"Looks like your height isn't working in your favor brother," joked Michael. "Well, it works in my favor most of the time, little brother," responded Morris, as he made his way toward the piano.
"So, this is the famous piano," he said.
"Famous sir?" Jimmy asked the Music Man.
"Well, more like the piano that my wife and I met at," the Music Man responded.
"But that's a story for another time."
"Come on, let's move this."
"Michael, you get the corner."
"Morris, you get the back, because you're the strongest.
"Jimmy, you get the other corner."

All four of them kneeled down and picked the piano up on each side accordingly, walking down the stairs.
Michael grunted from the weight of the piano. "My this is heavy."
Just as he said those words, he almost let go of the piano.

"Oh no!" shouted Jimmy.

Thankfully, Michael regained his composure and held on to the piano very securely.
"Thud"

The piano was successfully placed on the ground, in the Music Man's living room. The piano bench and stand were moved as well.
"Thank you boys," the Music Man said, as he reached into his pocket. "Here are two pounds."
"No sir, no need," said Morris.
 "It's always our pleasure to help."
"How about some tea?" asked the Music Man.

"Mother's got some on, she has cake remember?" said Morris.
"Oh yes."
"It's been a long morning," said the Music Man as he put on his hat.
 "Let's go get some cake!" shouted Michael.
"It's strawberry Cornelius, mother's special recipe!"
"You're going to love it my boy," said the Music Man to Jimmy.
Jimmy smiled in excitement.

"How many slices Corneeeelius?" asked Ms. Lois in a teasing manner. "This man, can eat an entire cake by himself."
Everyone laughed, including Jimmy.
"His wife used to try to get my secret recipe because he loves it so much." "But she sure could make some good pies."
Ms. Lois shook her head, in a sad manner.
"How long has it been?"
"Several years," said the Music Man.

"He looks like him, you know," said Ms. Lois.
"So, how did you two meet?"
"He..," the Music Man started to say.

"Ran away from home," interjected Jimmy.

The Music Man leaned back in his chair, surprised that he answered her question.
"Oh no," cried Ms. Lois.
"Aren't you worried that your mother may be looking for you?"
"No, she said it'd be easier if I weren't there," answered Jimmy.
"Oh honey, I'm sure she didn't mean that," Ms. Lois said in a low voice. Michael looked at his mother.
"Mother would have a fit if we left her."

"Their father passed away, many years ago," Ms. Lois said, as her eyes saddened. "I've had to raise them myself."
"They're good boys, they help me out so much."

"I've made just enough money working at the bakery, to send them off to get a good education."
"Their grandma helped teach them growing up, but then she passed."

"Now they can finally start their lives as men," said Ms. Lois as she smiled. The Music Man nodded in agreement.
"They've been my neighbors since my wife, child, and I moved into the house," the Music Man said, as he looked at Jimmy.
"You've done a fine job," he added, looking at Ms. Lois.

Ms. Lois smiled in acknowledgement of the Music Man's kind words.
"Well, we better be heading off," said the Music Man as he got up from his chair.
"The cake was delicious as always."
"Thank you so much."

"Thank you ma'am," said Jimmy.
"Anytime you two," said Ms. Lois.
Jimmy started to walk in front of the Music Man, and Ms. Lois whispered in the Music Man's ear.
"Make sure he goes back to his mother, she's probably distraught."
"I will," whispered the Music Man.
Michael, Morris, and Ms. Lois then said their goodbyes and off went Jimmy and the Music Man.

Chapter 5

Jimmy's mother's day at work went rather well. She was also a nanny for a wealthy family in the suburbs of London. One of the children had a birthday party and offered to give one of their toys to Jimmy. She was also given extra duties around the home, so she was able to get paid more. Jimmy's mother had very light brown skin with very pretty light brown eyes. She was taller in statue and had shoulder length dark brown hair. His dad was a handsome man with beautiful dark brown skin. Jimmy was a spitting image of both his mom and dad.
His mother showed up at their house and knocked on the door.
 "Jimmy."
There was no answer.
"Jimmy."
"Son."

"I have something for you."

Jimmy's mother couldn't afford to send him to school.

She taught him at night and he did chores around the house during the day. She started to feel uneasy as she pulled out her key to open the front door.
"Jimmy?"

His mother looked in every room in the tiny house but he was nowhere to be found.
Then, she found a note placed on his dresser.

Mother,

I know I make you sad so I'm going to leave now so that you can be happy. Please don't be sad, I don't want to make you sad anymore.

You should leave too and start a new life, it's what father would have wanted for you.

Jimmy's mother fell over and crumbled the paper.

"My son," she cried.

"You do make me happy."

"Please come back, I love you," she whispered to herself.

Chapter 6

The piano was a grand piano. It was black and shiny, Jimmy was mesmerized by it. The Music Man pulled a bench up to the piano and started to play. He sat up straight, hands placed in a relaxed manner on the piano keys. Jimmy nodded his head to the melody and started to hum. He couldn't believe how well the Music Man played.

He noticed how easily he got lost in his music. Jimmy sat back and listened. He started to daydream about his mother. He wondered if she had missed him and if she were looking for him. Suddenly, Jimmy's daydream was interrupted by a large thud in the kitchen.

"Hm," said the Music Man, as he got up and walked toward the kitchen. "Window wasn't closed all the way."

It was cold outside and the wind knocked over a book that stood on the counter. The Music Man closed the window and picked up the book.

He then added another piece of wood to the fire, and almost instantly, it became warm again.
"Want some more tea my boy?" asked the Music Man.
"Yes sir."

The Music Man poured two cups of tea and handed one to Jimmy. Jimmy took a sip and placed it on the table.
"Thank you," said Jimmy.

The Music Man then sat back down on the piano bench and began to play another piece.
"How did you become so relaxed sir?" Jimmy asked.
"Well my boy, my professor taught us."
"He told us to naturally let the music flow, to not force it."
The Music Man looked at Jimmy.
He noticed that Jimmy had a confused look on his face.
"Here."
"Sit up straight."
"And relax your hands."
"Would you like to play?" asked the Music Man.
"Of course, but I haven't had that much practice sir."
"You're not going to laugh at me, are you?"
"Of course not, I was once in your shoes," said the Music Man.
"Besides, no one is watching my boy."
"Come, have a seat."
Jimmy then took a deep breath and began to relax.
The music sheets were on the stand, but the Music Man had the pieces memorized.

He started to play another piece that was stored in his memory. Jimmy started to play along with him. It was to the Music Man's amazement that the young boy could play by ear.
"You are really good my boy, I had no idea."

A smile formed on their faces and they kept playing in harmony, as it was heaven to them.
"I think that's enough for now," the Music Man said, as he took his hands off the piano keys.
"It's almost midnight."

The Music Man looked at the clock above the fireplace, perplexed at the fact that they played for hours.
"May I keep playing sir?" Jimmy asked.

"You're not tired?" asked the Music Man in a joking manner.
"Not at all, playing music is fun to me," Jimmy replied, smiling.
"Well, alright."
"But keep it down."
"It has been a long day for me."

"Do you know how to read music?" asked the Music Man.
"No sir, it confuses me."
"I can just play out melodies."

"Music is a beautiful thing, isn't it?" the Music Man asked.
"Yes sir, yes it is."
"Well, I'm off to bed."

"Don't play too much," smiled the Music Man.

"You'll get a cramp in your hands."
"I won't!" Jimmy exclaimed.
The Music Man went off to bed and Jimmy continued to play.

The next morning, the Music Man awoke with a loud yawn and stretched, as he got out of bed.
Jimmy had fallen asleep at the piano.

"He played himself to sleep," whispered the Music Man to himself.

He then went over to Jimmy, picked him up off the bench and placed him on the couch.
He then sat down at the piano, and started to play another piece.

Jimmy awoke to the wonderful aroma of bacon and eggs again.

He raised his neck and smiled when he observed that the piano was still in its spot.

He then walked to the kitchen table and helped himself to breakfast.
"What was it like sir?" Jimmy asked, while picking up a piece of bacon.
"What was what like?" asked the Music Man.

"Playing music in front of everyone," Jimmy responded.
"Well, my first performance was frightening, to say the least," the Music Man replied.
"But I relaxed and just played."

"My first solo performance was the scariest, but my wife was there."
 "She sat in the front row."
"I can tell you really loved her," said Jimmy.
 "I did son, I still do."
"Have you written any songs about them?" Jimmy asked.
"Yes," the Music Man replied.
The Music Man looked down at his breakfast.

"I'm sorry to ask so many questions about them,"
Jimmy said, feeling bad.
"No, it's okay," the Music Man replied.

"We can play one of the songs after breakfast."
 Jimmy looked up and smiled.

The Music Man and Jimmy sat down on the bench in front of the piano.
 "I wrote this song after our son was born," the Music Man said, as he sat up straight.
"Forgive me, if I do not play it well."

He started to play the melody and Jimmy followed; both playing in harmony.
What happened next, was surely a mystery.

The piano and bench began to lift from the ground, spinning clockwise. "What's going on sir?!?" shouted Jimmy.
"I don't know my boy but hang onnnnnnn!" shouted the Music Man.

And before they could hold their breath, they ended up in another world.

Chapter 7

"Sir?"
"Where are we?" asked Jimmy.

"Why, I don't know," said the Music Man.
The Music Man looked around, dazed.
They were standing on a stage, in front of curtains.
"Stay here, I am going to go backstage."
The Music Man proceeded to the back of the curtain and lo and behold there were many instruments. There were violins, trumpets, and tucked in the middle was his piano.
"I am scared sir," whispered Jimmy, who was standing behind the Music Man.
"Surely there's an exit, I'll find out what's happening," said the Music Man. "Stay behind me and don't make a sound."
Jimmy gulped and stood behind the Music Man.

They began to walk, not knowing where they were going.

"Ah, there's an exit sign straight ahead," whispered the Music Man.

They made their way through the exit and walked down a flight of stairs. The Music Man stopped when he arrived at a door at the bottom of the stairs.

"Should we go out there?" asked Jimmy.

"Well we surely can't just stand here," the Music Man replied.

The Music Man then pushed the door open and the sun was shining in their faces.

"We're in another town!" shouted Jimmy in amazement.

"Look at the people, they're all smiling!" he added.

There were people from all walks of life who were different colors, walking amongst each other. In fact, the people were mixed with different shades of color. Some humans were very short and some were very tall. Some people had cars, and they looked very strange indeed. They were unlike any car that Jimmy had ever seen. However, mostly everyone was walking.

"I've never seen anything like this," said the Music Man.

There were shops throughout the town. There was a bakery, a candy shop, barbershop, salon, a butcher shop, amongst other shops. There was also a bank. The Music Man and Jimmy did not know which direction to take.

"Sir, what's happening?" asked Jimmy.

"I don't know son," the Music Man answered.

"Hey! Watch where you're going!" shouted a short little man.

The short little man was about four feet tall with a very large nose and large eyes. His skin was a mixture of orange and blue. He also had red freckles across his face. Jimmy presumed that the man was a dwarf. In fact, Jimmy noticed a lot of dwarves walking around.

"Oh I'm sorry Mr. Cornelius," the dwarf said.
"It's quite alright," said the Music Man.
"I have to get going but good luck!" shouted the little man as he ran off. "What a peculiar person," the Music Man said to himself. "And good luck?"

"Good luck with what?" he asked out loud.

"Sir, I don't think we're in the same world anymore," said Jimmy.
 "I can see that," said the Music Man.
"The question is."
"How did we get here?"
"And how do we get back?"'

"Where do you think we are?" asked Jimmy.

Jimmy and the Music Man looked around them and observed the town they were in.
There were also spirits walking with humans.

Jimmy noticed that people who were related had the same mixture of skin. He also noticed a man who had a green skin tone with teal blue mixed into it and the girl who was walking with him; had the same mixture.

The pets that some people owned were rather smaller or larger than usual. Dogs had distinct faces that Jimmy had never seen before. In fact, a lot of the people in the town had faces that he was not used to. However, they were all smiling, and that made Jimmy feel at ease.

"I think we're in another reality sir!" Jimmy shouted.

"Wherever we are, it's a lot different than our world," said the Music Man. "What is that beautiful sound?" he asked, out loud. It was a sound unlike he had ever heard before.

The Music Man looked to the left and right of him, nothing.
"Let's go this way," the Music Man instructed Jimmy.
They both followed the sound up until they reached a beautiful, green courtyard. They were taken aback at the sight they had seen.

A small orchestra of students, who were teenagers, were practicing music outside. In fact, they all stared at the Music Man at once.

Suddenly a young man who was about twelve or so stood up and spoke. "Sorry sir, I gathered everyone to come here and practice." "We're all just so excited."

"We want to perform really well."

"Sir what is he talking about?" asked Jimmy.
"I don't know son."
"I'm sorry, but you have the wrong person," said the Music Man.
"Continue doing what you were doing."

"'My apologies."

The students stared at the Music Man with an odd look on their faces.
 "He must be trying to trick us."
"To see if we get distracted," whispered the young boy to the rest of the students.
"Let's keep playing."
"Whatever it is that they are playing, is very beautiful," said the Music Man. "It sure is," agreed Jimmy.
"Come on," the Music Man said.

"Let's keep walking this way," he said as he continued to walk.

Suddenly Jimmy noticed a strange looking man leading a group of students into a school. In fact, the man and the students looked more like the people from the world Jimmy had come from.
The students obeyed the man's orders and looked straight ahead.

Jimmy had never seen soldiers in person before, but he imagined that they would walk like the students he was observing.

The man and the students entered the school quickly and quietly.
Suddenly, Jimmy noticed a young boy following them.
He didn't think that this boy was part of the group. In fact, the young boy was not a normal boy.
This young boy was a ghost, dressed in a tuxedo.
Jimmy took a step back and said,
"Sir, there's a..a..ghost."

"You mean a spirit?" asked the Music Man.
"I don't see anything," he added.
"No sir, the spirits we saw look peaceful and friendly."
"This was a ghost."
"Look," said Jimmy as he pointed.
"Where'd he go?" he asked.
"He was really pale."
"Sir, I have a bad feeling about this place."
"Can we leave?"
"Leave?" asked the Music Man.

"We must first figure out, how we arrived here," he added.
"Come on, let's keep walking."
Jimmy looked back at the school and proceeded to follow behind the Music Man.

Suddenly, a lady walked by them. The Music Man asked,
"Excuse me miss."
 "What is this place?"
"Why, this is Harmony Town," the lady answered.
"And we are the Harmonians."

"And.... you, are a famous conductor," she added.

"Why have you bumped your head and lost your memory sir?"
asked the lady. She stood about five feet and three inches tall.
She also had freckles with a mixture of purple and blue skin.
The Music Man just stood there, unable to speak.

"Can you please give us your name?" interrupted Jimmy.

"Well, my name is Antoinette Hummingfield."

"And I work over there at the bakery," as she pointed to her work.

"Oh," said the Music Man.

"How long have I been a conductor?" he asked.

"I'd say about a couple of years now."

"But now is not the time to have amnesia sir, competition has moved in!" she shouted.

"Competition?" asked the Music Man.

"Yes, his name is Jubilee Hornsbury," she said.

"He comes from up north I believe."

"With his own band."

"He's a real slender man, with a black mustache and very dark eyes."

"I heard he's quite good."

"He's a good conductor just like you but there's something very strange about him."

"He doesn't talk much, won't even look people in the eye."

"What year is it?" asked the Music Man.

"Why it's 2340 sir," Antwoinette answered.

"Matter of fact, nice outfit you have on there."

"How did we?" Jimmy started to say.

The Music Man just stared at the lady not knowing what to say.

"Sir! A spirit!" pointed Jimmy.

"That dress looks pretty on you," said the spirit to the person she was walking with.

The spirit was a young girl about in her twenties; she had purple skin with blue specks and long green hair.
"Oh, there are a few of those floating around here," laughed Ms. Hummingfield. "They're spirits that refuse to depart this world."
"They have chosen to stay with their loved ones." "I don't blame them."
   "So, if you see one, don't scream."
"They can't hurt you anyway."

"In fact, I think this is the only town that has some."
 "Then again, I've never ventured out of here."
"So, there very well could be more," she said with a wink.
Well, I have to run off now, my shift is about to start."
 "Good luck with your performance tomorrow!"
The Music Man and Jimmy looked at each other, both very confused.
 "You have a performance sir?" asked Jimmy in a nervous manner.
"I guess I do," the Music Man said nervously.

"Maybe I should go around town and ask some questions," he added. "What should I do?" asked Jimmy.
The Music Man reached into his pocket.

"Here, that should be enough to buy you some candy and or cakes from the bakery," the Music Man said, as he tossed Jimmy some shillings.
"Try and make a friend, the people in this town seem very nice," he added. The Music Man then looked at his watch.
"We'll meet back here in about two hours" he said.

"Alright, see you later sir!" Jimmy yelled, as he ran off.

The Music Man looked at Jimmy as he ran off.

Suddenly, a memory of his son appeared in his mind and he smiled.

He then spotted a short stubby man ahead standing outside of the butcher shop. The man wore thick glasses and was carrying a notebook of paper. "Excuse me, do you have a moment sir?" the Music Man asked.
"Well yes sir, I certainly do for you." the man said.
The man had teal skin with black hair.
"Have we met?" the Music Man asked.

"Well, my boy is one of your students," the man answered.
"Are you okay sir?" he asked.
"I think I may have an episode of memory loss," the Music Man said.

"Well, you have a concert tomorrow. Maybe you should go see the doctor sir."
"Christopher is very excited, he practices for hours," the man said.
"What is your name? It seems that I don't know it," the Music Man asked. "My name is William Mcclain."
"I'm a farmer."

"Doesn't look like you have any bruises on your head."
"Did you fall down sir?"
"It feels that way," said the Music Man in a joking manner.

"Your boy Chris, where is he now?" he asked.

"More than likely, at the candy store," Mr. McClain answered.
 "It's one of his favorite places to go to," he added.
"Well, I'll let you get back to your day. It was nice to have met you," said the Music Man.
William had a strange look on his face, but shrugged the Music Man's words off. The Music Man then decided he'll just play the part.

On the way to the candy store, Jimmy started to hum the piece that he and the Music Man played on the piano.
"I wonder how we got here," Jimmy thought out loud.
He suddenly thought about his mom.
In fact, this was the first time he thought about her since he arrived in this world.
"She's fine without me," he whispered to himself.
 "She hates me anyway."
Just as Jimmy muttered those thoughts to himself, he noticed a young boy and a woman hugging each other.
The boy looked about Jimmy's age, that is, his age in the other world. The woman hugging the young boy looked fairly young.
Jimmy felt sad at the sight.

He knew that the woman loved the boy very much.

Jimmy brushed the sad feeling off and hurried into the candy store.

Just as he was about to enter the store, the strange man he had seen before bumped into him.
He watched as the man hurriedly walked up the sidewalk.

"That must be who Ms. Hummingfield was talking about," he said to himself.
"Maybe I should follow him," he thought.
"Why young man, I haven't seen you here before," said a shorter, heavier man.
"I'm the owner of this shop,"
"Come on in."

Jimmy looked back at the strange man.
 "I'll see him again soon," he whispered to himself.
"We're kind of slow today," the man continued to say.
"With most of the teenagers preparing for the concert and all.
 "And the children?" pointed out the man.
"Their parents are very strict about their teeth becoming rotten."
 "But you look like you're about thirteen or so."
"Help yourself," said the man as he motioned Jimmy to the candy displays. "Where'd you move here from?"

"Surely you didn't come here alone."

"This town is very small, so everyone practically knows everyone."
 "Yes, I just moved here," said Jimmy, in a nervous tone.
The man kept talking while he was organizing a shelf of lollipops.

Jimmy ignored what the man was saying and started to browse the different kinds of candy.
He then noticed that along the wall, stood mirrors.
This was the first time Jimmy was able to look at himself.
"Interesting," said Jimmy.

Jimmy then pulled the change out of his pocket and counted it.

However, he realized that since they're in a different world, the same currency may not be used.
"Excuse me," said Jimmy as he approached the storeowner.

"Do you take these?" he asked, as he held out his hand full of shillings. The owner put on his spectacles and examined the currency.
"Hm, I don't know what those are, young man."

Jimmy turned away and went back to the candy, saddened that he could possibly not purchase any.

"There's so much to choose from!" exclaimed a young boy, about the same age as Jimmy. The boy was also around the same height. His skin was teal and he had orange and black hair. His eyes were green and he had a very youthful look to him.
"I come here at least twice a week."

"My dad says as long as I do my chores and behave, then I can have all of the candy I want," he laughed.
"My mom passed away, so it's just us."

"He just wants me to be happy I guess, as long as my teeth don't fall out!" "Name's Chris, Chris Mcclain," he said, as he reached to shake Jimmy's hand.

"My dad's a farmer, we live about two miles away." he added.

"My name is Jimmy, Jimmy Jakes," Jimmy said, introducing himself.

"Haven't seen you around these parts, who are your folks?" asked Chris.

A moment of silence had arisen, as Jimmy was unsure of what was happening. He remembered going to the Music Man's house and playing the piano. He then remembered suddenly being on the stage and then walking out of the building. However, the Music Man is known but he is not.

He then remembered the conversation that happened with Ms. Hummingfield. "Is there a conductor here in this town?" Jimmy asked.

"Why yes! I'm one of his students. We have a performance tomorrow actually," Chris answered.

"I feel bad, I skipped practice earlier."

"But there's another one in an hour."

"I need to go home and practice some more."

Jimmy noticed Chris's anxiousness.

"Do you play music too?" Chris asked.

"Yes, I can play by ear," Jimmy replied.

"That's so cool!" Chris exclaimed.

"How long has the conductor been in this town?" asked Jimmy.

"Hm, I would say for a few years now," Chris replied.
"I know that he's from another town."

"You may want to ask my father. If you want, you can come with me. He should be at the butcher shop," he added.
"I thought you said he's a farmer?" Jimmy asked.

"Well he is, and he actually sells meat to the butcher shop. I believe he's working on business with the owner," Chris replied.
"Well, would you like to come along?" asked Chris.

"Sure, why not," replied Jimmy, as he shrugged his shoulders.
He was taken aback by how nice Chris seemed.
"Come on,"
"Let's go!" said Chris excitedly.

Jimmy and Chris started to walk towards the butcher shop to try to get some meat.
"So, there's not many people here?" asked Jimmy.
"What do you mean?" asked Chris.

"I think there's a lot, but I'm sure it's the same as any other town."
"I do know this is the most peaceful town."
"Really?" Jimmy asked curiously.

"It doesn't get a name like Harmony Town for no reason," Chris replied. "There has only been one crime here."
"And that was because a little kid decided to steal a lollipop."

"So Mr. Borris makes sure to keep the lollipops right where he can see them."

"As far as the other candy, that's where the big mirrors come in."

"Then again, so that he can see everyone's reflections."

"I see," said Jimmy.

"There are also no fights and no beggars," Chris continued to explain.

"That sounds a lot different than where I'm from," said Jimmy.

"Really?" asked Chris.

"The only bad thing that does happen is that people get sick and die," Chris said.

"And that's why some people choose not to leave this world and stay as spirits."

"It sounds scary I know, but wouldn't you stay behind to be with your family as well?"

"Haven't thought about it," said Jimmy.

"So, what is your town like?"

"The town you came from," asked Chris.

"There's definitely crime, beggars, and people get sick and die too," said Jimmy.

"You didn't ever get scared?" asked Chris.

"No, my mom just always told me it's part of life."

"Well, be glad you're here now," said Chris as he wrapped his arm around Jimmy's shoulder.

"Nothing bad ever happens here."

Jimmy immediately thought about the strange man and the fact that Ms. Hummingfield said competition has moved in.
"What do you know about Mr. Cornelius?" asked Jimmy.

"He's very talented and moved here from some place a few years ago," Chris replied.

"He's a traveling conductor and composer but decided to stay here, because it's so peaceful."
Jimmy noticed another spirit, walking about.
"Don't be afraid."
"They can't hurt you," said Chris.
"They just don't want to leave."
"Yes, a lady told my uncle and I that," said Jimmy.
"Do you know any?" he also asked.
 "Any what?" asked Chris. "Spirits."
"No, but I bet it would be cool to meet one!" Chris said, with wide eyes.
"They keep to themselves."
"Is your mom a spirit?" Jimmy asked quietly.
"No," Chris answered in a somber tone.

"She just decided to leave, not sure why," he added.
Chris shrugged his shoulders.
Jimmy looked at Chris, and felt that his question saddened him.
"I'm so hungry," Jimmy said, trying to change the subject.
"Come on, let's get some sausages!" Chris exclaimed , as he ran to the butcher shop, hoping to see his father.

"Hi father, meet my new friend Jimmy!" Chris shouted as he ran through the shop.

"Chris, wait a moment, I am in the middle of a conversation," his father responded.

Chris had an impatient look on his face and decided to look around.

Jimmy also looked around the butcher shop, and noticed the selection of meats. He grew up poor so he didn't know the feeling of having too much.

His mom would feed him whatever she could scrape up. The cannery and part- time nanny job only paid his mom so much, and it was just enough to get by.

"Are you hungry?" Chris asked.

"Your mouth is watering!" he laughed.

"Yes," laughed Jimmy.

"But I don't have any money to buy anything."

"Don't worry, my father and the butcher are very good friends. We practically get the meat for free," Chris answered.

"Yes son, who do you have here with you?" asked William.

"He's my new friend. We met at the candy shop. His name is Jimmy," Chris replied.

"Well, how do you do son?" Mr. McClain asked, as he reached out his hand, expecting a hand shake.

"Where are you from?" he added.

Jimmy took a while to respond, as he didn't know exactly what to tell him.

"I'm from England sir," Jimmy said.

"Ah, haven't heard of it," Mr. McClain answered.
"Well, what do your parents do?" he asked.
Now Jimmy was really unsure as to what to say.

"I have been adopted by Cornelius Waters," Jimmy said.
"He's also the conductor here," he added.
"Well what do you know! I just spoke with him a while ago. He seemed a little confused," said William.
"Well boys, I have to run off home. Have some business matters to take care of in my study, " he added.
"Father, can we have some meat?" Chris asked.
 "The sausages look delicious."
"Sure, here you boys go." William said as he tossed a few coins to Chris. "You kids have fun and don't get into trouble," he added as he hurried off.
A wide smile appeared on Jimmy's face.

        The Music Man didn't know which way to go, as the town was very foreign to him. He walked past a shop and saw his reflection.
 He then spotted a slender man standing by a bench lighting up a tobacco pipe. "Excuse me sir, do you know where I can find Mr. Jubilee Hornsbury?" he asked the man.

The Music Man was suddenly taken aback because the mysterious man had very dark eyes. His eyebrows were arched as well, and mustache was much defined. His skin was a lighter shade of brown. He was also very tall. He did not look like the other people in the town.

He reached for his pipe, took it out of his mouth, and tipped his hat. "Why, that's me," he said, as he as he took a bow and said in a low voice.

The Music Man felt a strange feeling. As there was something disturbing about Mr. Hornsbury's mannerisms. They seemed almost sinister in nature.

"Um, well it was nice to meet you," said the Music Man as he backed up to turn the other direction.

"Are you Cornelius?" Mr. Hornsbury asked.

"Yes, I am," the Music Man said.

"Well, we'll be seeing each other around then," said Mr. Hornsbury with a sly smile.

Hornsbury then walked up the street and began handing out fliers to people. The fliers read...

"A concert you won't want to miss!"

The townspeople grabbed each flyer and showed excitement.

The Music Man turned around and walked the other way. The thought of Mr. Hornsbury's reactions and mannerisms made him feel very uneasy.

"So, you met Mr. Hornsbury." said a shorter woman standing by the fountain. She was very beautiful indeed. Her hair was long in length, brown, with a hint of gold. She had some of the most beautiful dark brown eyes, he had ever seen. Her skin was chocolate brown with orange mixed into it.

"Why, yes, I believe so," the Music Man said.

"Gives you the chills, doesn't he?" she asked.

"Indeed, I don't like him," the Music Man responded.

"It seems as if he's up to something," he added.

"I agree," the woman replied.

"My name is Olivia."

"Olivia Malani."

Her voice was really sweet, and the Music Man felt at ease.

"How do you do?" she asked as she extended her hand out for a handshake.

"I am fine, thank you," the Music Man said.

"I just moved back here about two days ago," Olivia continued to speak. "Where were you living before?" asked the Music Man.

"This town, 40 miles west," Olivia answered.

"I like it here more because it's so peaceful."

"And my sister needs help…"

"Sigh"

"I'm excited about the concert tomorrow," she smiled.

"I have loved music my entire life," she added.

"Me too, and I am the conductor that will be performing," the Music Man said.

"Really!?" Olivia exclaimed.

"You look like a conductor," she said in a joking manner.

Suddenly, she started to sing and the Music Man just stared in amazement.
He never heard a voice that was so beautiful before.
Not only was Olivia very pretty but her voice sounded so angelic.

Suddenly, his wife appeared in his head. He remembered how beautiful she looked when they first met. Then, a sad look appeared in his eyes and Olivia noticed it.
"Is everything okay?" she asked.

"Yes, um I have to get back to the school," the Music Man said, as he walked off. Olivia just stared at him, as he left.

The Music Man walked back to the school. Surprisingly, Jimmy and Chris were waiting at the side door in anticipation to start the rehearsal.
"Hello sir! I've been practicing a lot!" shouted Chris.

"Well that's good my boy, and you Jimmy?" asked the Music Man with a wink.
"Yes sir, there can never be enough practice", said Jimmy.
"Well, let's get to it!" the Music Man shouted while grabbing his hands together in excitement.

As they entered the auditorium, everything was set up on the stage. Almost every seat was filled. The Music Man looked at the

stage in confusion, as he didn't understand why he was there. He had experience with conducting music and was actually quite good, so he knew he could perform the piece well.
"I can't seem to find the music sheets," he said out loud.

"Sir they're right on the chair," said a young boy with red skin and green specks. He also had emerald green eyes.
The boy looked about fourteen years old.
"There are also copies in your office."
"How do you know this?" the Music Man asked, with a sound of confusion. "I helped write the music sir," the boy responded.
"Oh yes of course," the Music Man said, as he shook his head.
"Well thank you umm"
"Jacob sir," the boy said, with a confused look in his eyes.
"Is everything okay?"
"You've been acting strange."

"Yes, I'm fine, just have a mild case of amnesia," said the Music Man.
"I'll be okay."
The Music Man then stood at the podium and announced,
"Okay everyone, it's time for rehearsal."

Meanwhile, at the abandoned music school, Hornsbury was conjuring up a potion.
"I will be the best conductor ever."
"Everyone will listen to me."
Through my music!"

45

"Hahahahahaha," he said, as he laughed with an evil grin. Jubilee stirred the potion with much focus and determination. In his old town, Jubilee met a witch who was at the magic shop.

As, he could not naturally play music but he did love it. However, he had dark motives for wanting to play it.

He wanted to dominate the world, even if he had to use music to do so. The witch gave him a magic potion that could give him musical talent.

She also provided him with the recipe and chant for making more. In exchange for the magic potion; the witch grew younger. As, Hornsbury's soul became her's.

The witch did not know of Hornsbury's motives, as she didn't care. She mostly kept to herself.

Since then, Hornsbury has been on a mission to set up shop in every major town to possess everyone with his music.

Once the potion was done, he drank it without much hesitation. "Everyone will know who I am and the world will be mine!" "This is for all the people who laughed and ridiculed me!" "You will all be mine, and play for me!"

"Hahahahahaha," he shouted with an evil grin.

Hornsbury bowed and turned to look into the mirror. He then grabbed the sheet music off the table to go practice for rehearsal. He started to hum, his voice was very deep.

His students were much more submissive than the Music Man's. Some of the students could also sing. His band consisted of students playing instruments and singing as well.

They were indeed possessed and did everything Mr. Hornsbury requested. In his hometown, he held auditions and then would possess the individuals who were selected by playing the auditioning piece back to them. They then followed Mr. Hornsbury's orders to set up shop in Harmony Town.
His plan was to get everyone in the town to come to his concert.

"I wonder if the new conductor is any good," said Chris, as he and Jimmy were arranging their music.
"Father says his students are very talented," he added.
  "I have to practice and practice, but they somehow don't have to."
   "They just pick up their instruments and play."
"Father said that he overheard the students talking outside of the school." "He even thought that they somehow looked possessed," he added.

"Hey, do you want to go see them practice!?" he exclaimed.

"How? We have rehearsal now," Jimmy said in a serious manner.

"Afterward! We'll sneak in, I know a secret entrance. When I was little, my friends and I used to sneak in there all of the time. It's been abandoned for years, ever since I can remember. And I bet, that no one knows there's a secret entrance!"
"Want to go?!!!" Chris asked in an excited manner.
"I suppose so," said Jimmy.

"Should we tell my uncle?" Jimmy asked.

"No, it'll be our secret," Chris said, while putting his finger to his lips. "Besides, don't you think it's odd, that they came here, of all places?" he added.
"Well isn't my uncle one of the best conductors?" Jimmy asked.
"Yes, but why did Mr. Hornsbury come HERE?" Chris asked.

"I would think to compete," Jimmy said, as he shrugged his shoulders. "Hmmm, maybe so, but why?" Chris asked.
"I guess we'll try to find out," said Jimmy.

Luckily, for Chris, their rehearsal started before Mr. Hornsbury's and was finished quickly.
"Come on, let's go!" Chris said excitedly.

"Boys, where are you off to?" the Music Man asked.
"Um," Jimmy couldn't lie to the man who took him in.
"We were just going to get some ice cream," answered Chris.
Jimmy looked to the side, but the Music Man did not notice.

"Well, don't be too long. I'm sure your father wants you back home before late," the Music Man said.
"Try not to get into trouble," he added.

He then turned around, to gather his belongings.

"Good rehearsal everyone. We have one more before the big performance. See you all tomorrow," announced the Music Man, to the rest of the orchestra.

"Sleep well," he added.

Jimmy and Chris then hurried off to catch Mr. Hornsbury's rehearsal.

"Come on! Before we miss them!" shouted Chris to Jimmy, as they were running. Chris and Jimmy went behind the building and there was a side door that was partially hidden.

When the school was remodeled, the workers did not notice the hidden door.

"This is it," said Chris.

He was not nervous at all. In fact, he seemed excited.

"I think this is the entrance," Chris said.

Jimmy gulped, for he knew that they weren't supposed to be there.

"Let's just have a peep and then leave," said Jimmy in a nervous tone.

Jimmy and Chris quietly tiptoed down the halls, not knowing which direction to take.

The school was dark, and the halls were long and narrow.

"Do you know where the stage is?" whispered Jimmy.

"I can't tell, it's so dark," said Chris.

"This was a bad idea," said Jimmy.

"I think it's this way," said Chris.

All of a sudden, they heard footsteps and humming. It was Mr. Hornsbury, walking to his dressing room. Chris looked at Jimmy and motioned to follow him.

As Mr. Hornsbury entered his room, he took off his robe and looked into his mirror.

"Everyone will know my name!"

He looked at the potion and shouted, "There's more where that came from!" he added.

Chris and Jimmy both looked at each other in fright.

Suddenly they knew, that Mr. Hornsbury was planning something wicked and evil. They then turned away and ran as fast as they could.

Mr. Hornsbury was too consumed with his magic to notice that he was being watched.

"Come on!" shouted Chris.

"We have to go tell your uncle!"

As the Music Man was walking from the music school, Chris's father bumped into him.

"You're walking the wrong way Cornelius...your home is that way."

"Remember, it's the white house with the wrap around porch," said William. "Thanks William, it's the amnesia," the Music Man said as he shook his head. Then, as the Music Man walked towards his house, he spotted Olivia sitting on a bench. She

looked like she was thinking very hard. They talked for about a hour and the Music Man instantly fell in love with her.
"Would you like to come to dinner after my performance tomorrow?" asked the Music Man.
"Yes."

"Of course Cornelius," Olivia answered with a wide smile.

Suddenly, Chris and Jimmy came running to them, and ranting. Both boys were breathing really hard.
"Calm down boys," said the Music Man.

"Take a deep breath, and tell me what is going on."

"It's Hornsbury sir," said Chris, panting.

"He's plotting something very wicked."
"It's true sir," said Jimmy.
Olivia made a nervous sound.

"What should we do?" Jimmy asked.

"Well, we're going to go home and think," the Music Man said.
"I can't," said Chris, still trying to catch his breath.
"It's way past dawn."

"Father wants me back home, I will see you all tomorrow!" he shouted, as he started to run home.
"Please tell me what you all come up with!" he added.

Jimmy stayed in front of the Music Man and Olivia, as he did not know which way home was. Or if he even had a home, for that matter.

"Sir, do you know which way home is?" Jimmy asked.

"It is that way," pointed the Music Man.

"It's a white house with a wrap- around porch."

"Thank you sir!" said Jimmy, as he started to run.

As Jimmy ran, he bumped into Mr. Hornsbury and was immediately frightened. Suddenly, Jimmy thought that he knew that they watched him. "Are you lost lad?" Mr. Hornsbury asked. "No sir, I'm just trying to find my way back home," said Jimmy.

"And I'm rather sleepy."

"Oh, you're in Cornelius's band," said Mr. Hornsbury. "Yes, I am. I have to go now," Jimmy said nervously. "Why surely you have a moment," Hornsbury smiled. "Want to hear a snippet of what we'll be performing?"

"That's alright, I really have to get going," said Jimmy nervously.

Not sure of why Mr. Hornsbury would even invite him, but then suddenly Jimmy remembered that Chris said the students are probably possessed and maybe, just maybe he wants to possess him as well!

Jimmy then ran off but looked back and Mr. Hornsbury was staring at him with dark, evil eyes.

Jimmy shuddered and continued to run.

Jimmy immediately found the house. It was large, indeed with a wrap-around porch. To his surprise, the door was already opened. He quickly turned on the lights and waited for the Music Man.

"Which way, my dear?" the Music Man asked Olivia.

"Well, it's about three blocks from here. I'm sure you're tired," Olivia responded. "I can manage," she added.
"Oh no, it's fine, it's dark, " insisted the Music Man.

"And if they're right about him, who's knows what he's planning," the Music Man added.
"Well, if you insist," said Olivia, with a smile.
 "So, what happened to Jimmy's parents?"
"If I may ask."

"Well, his dad died and his mom doesn't want him anymore," said the Music Man.
"Well that's nice of you to take him in. He seems like a really good boy," Olivia said.
"Oh yes, indeed. He's really gifted too, he can play music by ear," said the Music Man.
"Really?" Olivia asked.

"How wonderful, I can't wait for the performance tomorrow," she added. "Well, there's home," Olivia said as she stopped walking.
"Good luck with your performance, I will be there," she added.
"Thank you, I hope you enjoy it," the Music Man said.

"Dinner after the concert tomorrow?" he also asked.
"Of course," Olivia smiled.
She then leaned forward, to kiss him on the cheek.

The Music Man smiled and stared at her as she walked to her house.
He forgot which house was his, and it was almost pitch black outside.

He looked around and just walked the same way they came from.
"I think this is it," the Music Man said to himself.
He knocked on the door and sure enough, it was his home, as Jimmy opened the door.
The Music Man sighed in relief.

He looked at the rooms, and admired the beauty the house possessed. The kitchen was large with a very comforting living room.
"What are we going to do sir?" asked Jimmy.
"Everyone thinks we are from here," he added.
"What has happened?"
"I'm sure my mom is worried sick."

"I ran away, but I feel so bad for leaving without saying goodbye."
"What if we're stuck here forever?" he said as he panicked.
"Well, let's think," the Music Man said in a calming voice.

"What is the last thing you remember before we ended up here?" he asked. "Well, we were playing your piano."
"And then it started spinning."

"But I can't remember after that," said Jimmy.

"I think we have to play the piano!"

"Mr. Hornsbury scares me and I tell you sir, he is planning something wicked," said Jimmy in a frightening tone.

"We have to stop him!"

"Well, let's just handle him first," the Music Man said.
"And then we'll try to get back home," he added.
"Ok, do you promise, that we'll get back home?" asked Jimmy.
He didn't know why, but he suddenly missed his mom.
"Just want to make sure my mom's okay, she's alone," he added.

"Of course, I will try my hardest to get us back home," the Music Man assured.
"Now you get some rest."
"We have a big day ahead of us."

The Music Man then lead the way up the stairs.
"Ah, there's a bedroom," the Music Man noticed.
"Sir...what about clothes?" Jimmy asked.
"Sleep in your clothes tonight," the Music Man answered.
"You can go buy some tomorrow."
"I'll make sure to see how I can convert my money."
"Good night, my boy."
"Good night," said Jimmy.

Jimmy started to weep as soon as the door was shut.

He found a pen and notebook in his room and thought of just writing to his mom. He didn't care if she had seen it or not, he just wanted to write his feelings down.

Mom,
I miss you very much.
I will come home soon. I know you love me.
And we will be a happy family.
Love,
Jimmy.

Jimmy put the piece of paper down on the nightstand, rolled over, and went to sleep.
The Music Man opened the door to check on him.
"Ah, he's sound asleep," he said to himself.
"What's this?"
The Music Man noticed the piece of paper on the night stand, picked it up, and read it. There was also an address on it.
"This must be his address."

"Maybe if I play that song, I can go back."

Suddenly, the Music Man grabbed it and went immediately to the school.

He was given a spare key to enter, so he made his way backstage.

And there, still sitting in the middle, was his piano. The Music Man had the music piece memorized.
He pulled a bench at the piano and started to play.

The piano then began to spin, and the Music Man went back to the other world.
"Wow!"
"It worked!" he shouted.

The Music Man checked his home and everything was still intact.
He even looked at himself in the mirror.
"Wow this is interesting!"

"Let's get you delivered," he said to the piece of paper.

He put the letter in an envelope and addressed it with Jimmy's address.
"It shouldn't be too long for you to get delivered."
As Jimmy's home wasn't too far.
"Don't worry Misses Jakes."
"Jimmy will be home soon."
The Music Man then put the letter in his mailbox and traveled back.

Chapter 8

Jimmy awoke with a cramp in his foot from running the night before. "Sir, we're still here," Jimmy said as he limped to the kitchen.

"Why yes, yes we are. And today's the big day!" The Music Man stated as he grabbed his hands in excitement.

"What about Mr. Hornsbury?" Jimmy asked.

"I'm telling you sir, he's plotting something evil. His eyes are so dark sir, he frightens me," he added, as he shivered.

"Well, as long as you're near me, nothing will happen to you. I will make sure of that," assured the Music Man.

"That lady you we were with is very pretty," Jimmy said in a tired voice as he ate his porridge.

He looked up and smiled at the Music Man. "Ah yes, indeed she is," the Music Man said.

"But, we will be leaving soon. It will be short-lived," he added with a sad look in his face.

"But that doesn't have to be sir, maybe she could come with us!" shouted Jimmy. "I don't think so, she's not part of our world," said the Music Man.

"Bummer," Jimmy said, in a disappointing manner.

"Well enough sad talk, I'm off to the school. Go meet up with Chris. I'm sure you two can get in some kind of trouble," the Music Man said.

"Don't forget, rehearsal is in two hours," he added. "Ok sir! See you soon!"

Jimmy then ran off to try to find Christopher's farm.

He remembered the description he give him. Sure enough, he found it.

The farm was very large. There were cows, chickens, roosters, as well as horses. However, the animals also looked strange. Jimmy knocked on the front door, in hopes that Chris was up. The sun had just come up but that didn't stop Jimmy. He wanted to make sure that Mr.

Hornsbury was stopped in time.

To Jimmy's satisfaction, the door opened, and Chris's dad answered.

William McClain had a cup of coffee in one hand, and wiping his eye with the other.

"Why Jimmy, it's really early," said Mr. Mcclain, as he yawned. "Is everything okay?"

"Yes sir," replied Jimmy. "We just have to practice."

"Oh, I see," Mr. McClain said. "Well come in, come in," he added. "Let me wake Chris up for you."

"Would you like some tea and biscuits while you wait?"

"Yes sir, thank you," said Jimmy with excitement. "He should be down in a minute," Mr. McClain said.

Jimmy looked around and he noticed pictures of Chris's mom with him when he was a little boy. He thought to himself that she was a beautiful woman. He also wondered why she didn't stay as a spirit. He noticed that their house was quite cozy and warm. Suddenly, a sad feeling came over Jimmy.

For he realized that Chris would not be able to come with him when they go back into their world.

"Are you ready!?" "I'm so excited!" Chris shouted from the top of the stairs.

Chris's father laughed, with his arms folded. "Chris does nothing but practice."

"I'm excited too, but what about Mr. Hornsbury?" asked Jimmy.

"What about Mr. Hornsbury?" asked Chris's father, out of curiosity. "Well, father, we caught him talking to himself," replied Chris.

"He was brewing up some kind of potion," he added.

"I knew he looked like he was up to something," said Chris's father. "But I don't want you all going to him by yourselves."

"I don't want you all getting hurt, we don't know what he's capable of." "I'll talk to some townspeople to see if they know anything."

"However, you all must focus on this concert," he said.

"It could be that, he's trying to compete with your instructor."

"We'll get to the bottom of it afterward."

"Now hurry along, the earlier you are there, the better. Can't wait to hear you both play!" Chris's father shouted in excitement.

Chapter 9

Jimmy and Chris ran off to the school, eager for the concert. "I sure hope I don't mess up, I'm quite nervous!" yelled Chris, as he held on to his instrument.

Chris ran much faster than Jimmy.

He wanted so much to make his father proud. Chris and his father didn't have a bad relationship but Chris wanted to have his father know of his abilities.

"Well, I'm sure you'll be fine, I'm the one who's nervous," said Jimmy. "Haven't practiced that much," he added.

"I just got here!"

"I can play by ear but still, it would be nice to practice more," he added. "Well thankfully, we're not the only two playing," Chris laughed. Chris and Jimmy entered the auditorium, and everyone was in their seat ready to rehearse.

The Music Man was nicely dressed in a tuxedo. The tailor made sure to hand deliver it.

The Music Man was still taken aback by everything that had occurred.

Jimmy looked at him in amazement, for some reason it made him feel at ease that the Music Man was so calm.

"Excuse me, may I sit next to you?" asked a beautiful young lady. She was holding a violin, and her hair was light brown, with reddish orange streaks. She also had brown dreamy eyes. Her skin was dark brown with light brown specks. Jimmy did not mind that she looked so different from him. In fact, he thought she was prettier than some of the girls from his world. Her smile was even contagious.

"I usually sit over there," she pointed.

"But I'm having a little trouble hearing this morning, and I want to be able to hear," she added.

"That's fine by me, this seat's available," Jimmy said after he cleared his throat. "I'm also playing the violin, so I don't think it will matter."

Jimmy was only 13 years old, but he knew what beauty looked like. He smiled at her and placed her music sheet on the stand for her. "Name's Jimmy," said Jimmy.

"Nice to meet you. My name is Soriya." "My name's Chris!" shouted Chris.

"Ah, I remember you, from the first day of practice," said Soriya.

"Is this your first concert?" she asked Jimmy out of curiosity.

"Yes, yes it is," he said.

"How about yourself?" Jimmy asked.

"Same, my parents are really excited," she said. Jimmy suddenly felt sad again.

He wished his mom were there to listen to him play.

The Music Man noticed the sad look on Jimmy's face and made his way to him. "Are you all ready?" he asked.

"I am!" shouted Chris.

"I've practiced all night!" shouted Chris.

"And you Jimmy? I know you haven't been able to practice that much," the Music Man said.

"Yes, I am," Jimmy said as he smiled at the Music Man with excitement in his eyes.

He knew that the Music Man cared deeply for him, and he didn't want to upset him by being sad.

"Good," the Music Man responded. "I'm glad to see that the seats are full."

"Have had a couple of students not being able to make it."

The students really didn't know each other, as they introduced themselves the first day of practice, but after that it was all about practicing and getting ready to perform.

"We're going to practice one more time."

"And then our guests shall be arriving soon," the Music Man said.

"I wonder, how many people do you think are coming?" asked Chris.

"Well, I spoke with the tailor. He said it's supposed to be rather full," the Music Man replied.

Jimmy could not understand how the Music Man was able to pretend so well. He admired him for being so brave and also for his positive attitude.

"Speaking of which, time for practice," the Music Man added. "I'm sure you all will do well."
He bowed and smiled at Jimmy with a wink.

The Music Man then started to talk to the other students.

"Right after we're done, we're going to see what Mr. Hornsbury is up to!" shouted Chris.
"Shhh!" whispered Jimmy.

"Who's Mr. Hornsbury?" asked Soriya. "He's the other conductor," said Chris. "He came from another town."
"He's in the old school with his students." "His concert is in a couple of days."
"But he's planning something evil," said Chris.

"Ohhh so that's who my dad was talking about," said Soriya. "And what exactly are you all going to do?" she asked.
"Well, I was thinking we would try to destroy the potion that he was drinking out of," Chris replied.
"We can sneak in his dressing room when he's not there," Chris said. "Want to know a secret?" Soriya whispered.
"Angela, she's a few rows back, knows the school inside out." "I remember her telling me there's a secret passage."
"There are more secret passages?" Chris asked. "I thought there was only one?" he added.
"I don't know but she used to always play in the school," Soriya responded. "All four of us can go and she can lead the way," she added.

"There's only one problem," said Jimmy. "What about Mr. Hornsbury?"
"Where will he be?" he asked.

"We don't even know what he's planning," he added. "Well that's why we need to get there quickly," said Chris.
"Besides, whatever he's planning, I have a feeling, it involves people," he said. "And everyone will be there, his concert isn't for another few days."
"Sounds like a plan, I'll be right back. I'm going to tell Angela," said Soriya. "Great, now there are girls involved. We don't know what we're getting into," Jimmy said nervously.

"Well someone has to stop him," Chris said.

"And her friend knows of a secret passage," he added.

Chris checked his instrument to make sure it was finely tuned.

"Okay, if you say so," said Jimmy.
"We're in," winked Soriya as she returned back to her seat. Jimmy laughed nervously.

The orchestra practiced one more time. Jimmy, Soriya, and Chris all played the violin. Soriya's friend, Angela, played the flute. The rest of the orchestra played the viola and cello.

Guests began to arrive. Jimmy was amazed at how many people were showing up. Jimmy took a deep breath. The Music Man made his way to the podium, and Jimmy looked up at him.

"Attention."

"We are now ready to begin," said the Music Man loudly.

"Please, everyone. Be seated."

The orchestra sounded lovely. Jimmy could easily play the violin. He was so amazed at how well the Music Man conducted. Chris also played wonderfully and with much confidence, which surprised Jimmy.
Jimmy looked at Soriya and noticed that she was passionate about playing music. She kept her eyes on her music sheet without looking away and made sure the stand held up firmly. After observing the others, Jimmy remained focused and continued to play.
"I love music," he said to himself.

The performance received a standing ovation.

The Music Man took a bow, thanked and released the orchestra.

Chapter 10

"I'm going to go get Angela," said Soriya. "Where should we meet at?"

"Let's meet by the side door," said Chris.

Soriya nodded and quickly gathered her instrument.

The teens hugged their parents, while Jimmy hugged the Music Man. "You did a very good job," the Music Man said in a proud voice. "You too sir!" exclaimed Jimmy.
"Well off you go," said the Music Man. "Be careful!" he added.
The four teens then hurried off and met up at the side door. "Hey guys, this is Angela," said Soriya.
Angela was about the same height as Soriya, only her hair was shorter. She had dimples and light brown eyes. Her skin was a mixture of green and blue with purple specks; she too was beautiful.
"Hi I'm Chris," Chris said. "Jimmy," Jimmy said.
"So you know the ins and outs of the school?" asked Chris. "Sure do!" said Angela.
"My dad was a construction worker there, and I used to play there sometimes."

"Well, we better get going," said Chris. "There's no time to waste," he added.

The four teens ran to the school. It was dawn, so they still had daylight. Angela led the three to a hidden passage that had two directions. It was very dark. "Let's split up," said Chris.
"Jimmy and Angela go that way," he added. "And Soriya and I will go this way."

"The main thing is, we need to get that potion." "So if you can, break it."

"Where should we meet back up?" asked Jimmy.

"If we don't run into each other here," replied Chris. "Then we can meet up at the other school."
"At the side door."

The teens nodded their heads.

Jimmy and Angela started walking. "There are so many doors," said Angela. "How do we know which one is Mr. Hornsbury's?"
"Shh," said Jimmy. "You hear that?"
Angela shook her head no.

There were footsteps, which became louder and more distinct.
"That's him!" whispered Jimmy.
He pointed to a shadow that turned a corner down the hall.

Jimmy and Angela quickly followed the shadow; while trying not to be heard. They followed Hornsbury to his dressing room. Hornsbury entered and slammed the door shut. Angela and Jimmy both put their ears to the door. "Enjoy this Cornelius!" "Enjoy it while it lasts!" "I will steal the show in a couple of days and EVERYONE will know who I am."
"And once they are possessed, I will control them and then I'll go to the next town until I rule the world!"
The two teens, Jimmy and Angela, heard this and became very scared. They then ran back to find Chris and Soriya.

Meanwhile, Soriya and Chris fell down a shoot to the basement.

"I think this is where Hornsbury's orchestra is sleeping at," said Soriya. "See, look."

"Their uniforms are laid out and they're all matching." "There is definitely something going wrong here." "Everything matches...even their shoes!" shouted Chris. "Shhh!" Soriya said. "They could be down here."

All of a sudden Chris and Soriya heard music.

"They're in the auditorium!" Soriya shouted.

The students were rehearsing and there was distinct singing as well.

"Come on!" "Let's see what else we can find!" said Chris.

"Oh look!"

"Someone left their necklace," said Soriya. "Well, it's all dirty."

"Wait, there are initials on it," she added. "JM"

"What do you think it stands for?!" she asked.

"Beats me," Chris said with a shrug of his shoulders.

Soriya was naturally curious. She came from an interesting family. Her father was the town officer and mother, the town clerk.

Her dream was to become a detective one day. "And why would it be left here?" she asked.

"Well, I'm sure the orchestra sleeps here," Chris said.

"Look, there are cots," Chris said as he pointed to an open room. "Yuck, I couldn't imagine sleeping in those!" said Soriya. "Well, maybe they're not really themselves," Chris said.
"I get the feeling that they're possessed Soriya," Chris said.

"Really? Maybe we should leave," Soriya said, with a scared look on her face.

"What if he finds us?" she asked nervously. "Well, I won't let that happen," Chris responded.
"We should leave now, and try to find Jimmy and Angela," he added. "Should we take the necklace?" asked Soriya.
"No, then they'll know someone was here," Chris replied.
"Whoever owns the necklace, you know," he added.
Soriya nodded but then she noticed Chris's hand was balled into a fist. She didn't think any of it.
She followed Chris as they tried to find the basement door.

"Shhh, we have to walk quietly," said Chris as he walked in front of Soriya. Luckily, the two teens could still hear the music.
"Look."

"I think this is it," Chris said.

Suddenly, Soriya screamed while holding her mouth.

Chris turned and looked at her.

She was pointing at a shadow near the doorway to the sleeping room.
He stood in front of her.

"Wait here, I will go check it out," he said.

"Chris, what if it's Hornsbury?" Soriya whispered, while trembling.
"I won't let him hurt you," Chris whispered.
"Chris, I'm scared."
"Shh," said Chris.

Suddenly Soriya's teeth were grinding.

"Why have you come here?" a voice whispered. Soriya screamed again.
"I won't hurt you but you should leave now!" shouted the image.
"What are you?" stuttered Chris.
"I am one of his victims," the image said.
  "Whose victim?" asked Chris.
  " Hornsbury's."
Suddenly the image became more distinct and it was a young boy, dressed in a tuxedo.

His skin was pale, his hair brown. "Hornsbury put a spell on me," said the boy. "But the spell didn't work on me," he added. "We had a concert in another town,"
"I tried to stop him from proceeding."

"But, he locked me away in a closet door in the auditorium."

"After the concert, he came back and put a spell on me, which basically killed me," he added as he looked down.

"But, as you see, I am now a ghost." "And I have been following him."
"He's trying to take over the world, and possess every soul," he said. "I knew it!" shouted Chris.
"How do you know this?" Chris also asked.

"The night before the concert, I followed him, he was meeting the witch who gave him the potion," responded the boy.
"It gives him magical abilities."

"And when one drinks the potion, it can last for four hours."

"She also helped him put a spell on the auditioning pieces, which is how he was able to possess us."
"But once the potion is gone; all of his magical abilities will disappear." "She gave him a wand too but he only used it when he was possessing us." "I suspect he's also going to use it at his performance."
"To possess people." "Oh no," said Soriya. "Yeah."

"He must have seen me, because the following day, he put the spell on me." "I miss my parents and little brother."

A tear dropped from his eye.

"I am going to help you stop him before he does the same thing in this town," he added.
"What is your name?" Chris asked. "Name's Phillip," the boy said.
"What do we do now?" asked Soriya. "The music has stopped," she added.
"Come on, there's a secret passage," said Phillip. "Oh wow, there's another one?" asked Chris.

"There are about five I think," said Phillip.

Phillip led them to a closet, and sure enough behind the old costumes, there was a door.
"I wonder why there are so many passages," said Chris. "Well this school was built many years ago," said Soriya. "Do you think it was used in a war?" asked Chris.
"There were wars in this town?" asked Phillip. "That seems odd," he added.
"Yes, a long time ago," Chris answered. Chris focused back on their plan.
"Phillip, where does this lead to?" asked Chris. "It leads to the back of the school,"
said Phillip.

"Don't worry, we're safe," he added.

"How do you know about all of these?" Chris asked.

"When you're a ghost, you have nothing but time to explore," responded Phillip. "Does it feel weird, being a ghost?" Angela asked with a gulp.

"I feel nothing, but I do have memories," said Phillip. "I have all of my memories," he added.

"Well, once we stop Mr. Hornsbury, we'll try to bring you back to life," said Chris.

"Thanks guys, I really hope we stop him, he's very powerful," said Phillip. "Don't worry, we will," said Chris.

The teens finally exited the back door and stood outside. "I wonder where Jimmy and Angela are," said Soriya.

"Let's just go back outside where we're supposed to meet at," said Chris.

Jimmy and Angela were still searching for Chris and Soriya. The hidden halls were confusing for them, as they didn't know which way to travel. "Hmmm I wonder where this hall takes us," said Angela.

"Shoot, I think we're lost," she added.

"Well, let's just not give up. Let's try this way," said Jimmy.
Sure enough, Jimmy found the way out to the back door. "Boy are we glad to see you two!" shouted Angela.
Suddenly, Angela froze up, pointed, and stuttered, "who-who-who's that?" as she was pointing at Phillip.
"Name's Phillip, I won't hurt you."

Angela tried to touch him, and as expected, her fingers went through him. "Did that hurt?" she asked.

"No, I'm a ghost," Phillip said as he laughed.

They all started laughing.

"He's going to help us stop Mr. Hornsbury," said Chris. "He was practically murdered by him," he added.

"He's a very evil man and he will pay for what he has done," said Phillip very loudly.

"Yes, we heard his plan," said Jimmy.

"He's going to try to possess everyone, and take over the world," he added. "Well that's not going to happen, not if I can help it," said Phillip.

Phillip was very upset, he wanted to have his life back. "We will stop him," Phillip said.

"Well then, let's get to it," said Chris as he grabbed his hands.

"Well, what do we do?" asked Soriya.

"What's the plan?" she also asked. "Let's meet up with my uncle."

"He'll know what to do," said Jimmy.

Chapter 11

The Music Man and Olivia were together at his house. He had fallen in love with her beauty and mind.

"I could talk to you for hours," he said to her.

He had made her some tea and she brought over a cake to celebrate his performance.

"So, where are the children?" asked Olivia.

"Well, Jubilee is not what people think he is," he said.

"I remember them saying that they caught him saying some words," said Olivia. The Music Man nodded his head and took a sip of his tea.

"Well, I haven't seen them since the performance," the Music Man said. "I presume they're trying to stop him."

"I see," said Olivia.

The Music Man then grabbed a piece of cake.

Olivia started to sing again and the Music Man started to go into a trance.

"You have such a beautiful voice," he said under his breath.

All of a sudden, Olivia stopped singing.

"Well, I have to head off. My sister needs help again with sewing," she said as she stood up.

"See you tomorrow?" she asked, as she gathered her things.

"S..s…sure!" the Music Man exclaimed.

Olivia quickly left out the front door.

The Music Man was taken aback that she left so fast.

"Busy woman," he said to himself.

"Hm," he said as he poured some more tea.

He shrugged his shoulders but felt very strange. He then shook the feeling off.

Suddenly the door slammed open.

"Sir! We know what he wants to do!" shouted Chris.

"Slow down, slow down boys. Take a deep breath," said the Music Man. "We know what he's up to now," said Chris, barely catching his breath. "He's trying to possess everyone through his music."
He added, while he was kneeling over. "Is this true?" asked the Music Man. "Yes, I'm afraid it is sir," said Jimmy. "Here, meet Phillip," said Chris.
"He'll tell you everything," he added.

"I don't see anyone, only you two boys and girls," the Music Man said jokingly. Suddenly, the Music Man's expression turned into a blank stare.
"Is that a...?" asked the Music Man.

"A ghost, yes. My name is Phillip," he said. "I am Cornelius."
"How does it feel to be a ghost?" the Music Man asked. "I don't feel anything, but I wish I could," said Phillip.
"Being alive was truly a gift," Phillip added.

"Well, you will be soon!" said Chris with anger. "What's the plan sir?" asked Jimmy.
"What should we do?" he added.

"Hm, I'm not sure," the Music Man said. "What do you mean?" asked Chris.
"Well, if he is as evil as you all are saying he is ... then I think we should be very careful. We don't know what all he's capable of," said the Music Man.

"But we must do something and fast," said Chris in an impatient tone. "I'll ask Olivia and see what she thinks."
"In the meantime, just try to calm down. The concert isn't for another couple of days,"
"There is time," said the Music Man.

"Sir, may I speak with you for a moment?" asked Jimmy in a quiet tone. "Sure," said the Music Man.
"In private," said Jimmy very quietly, as he was looking down.
"We'll just go outside," said Chris sarcastically.
"I'm sure people who walk by your house won't be alarmed that there's a ghost standing outside," said Chris.
"He doesn't look like the other spirits, you know."

Soriya and Angela then chuckled. "Just go out back," said the Music Man. "There's a shed that's empty," he added. "We'll sweat!" yelled Chris.
Chris was the aggressive one out of the children. He was raised solely by his dad, didn't really know how to be anything but give or take orders. "Besides, what's so important anyway?"
"Why can't we all talk about this, Jimmy?" asked Chris in a direct manner. "Chris, let's just go out back," said Soriya.
"If Jimmy wants to talk in private, I'm sure it's important," she added. Jimmy looked at her and smiled.
"Thank you young lady," said the Music Man. "Come on guys," said Soriya.

"He seems very upset," said the Music Man, referring to Chris.
"Yes, he's not too happy about Phillip."

"Hornsbury put a very powerful spell on him sir," said Jimmy, with a sad look on his face.
"It was very cruel," he added.

"I am scared sir, none of us knows anything about magic." Jimmy then sighed and thought for a moment.

"I think we just need his spell book."

"If we get that, we can stop him," he added. "I'll try to come up with a plan."
In the meantime, I'll try to persuade the people of this town not to go to his concert," the Music Man said.
"Okay! We'll meet back here tonight," said Jimmy.

"Sounds like a plan my boy, be careful," the Music Man said.

Jimmy rushed out back to the shed and told the others what they must do. "Okay guys, this may get a little tricky. We need to get his spell book," said Jimmy.
"Wait, how could we possibly know where that is?" asked Chris.
"Well wouldn't it be in his dressing room?" asked Angela.
"No, he wouldn't put it somewhere it could be found easily," said Chris. "He probably keeps it on him at all times," he said.
"That doesn't make sense, someone would see it," said Soriya.
Jimmy looked at her, "She's right, we would've noticed it." "What if it's a little book?"
asked Chris.

"Maybe there isn't a book, maybe he memorized certain spells," he added.

"Know what I think?" asked Angela. "I think we're all wrong."

"I don't think we're looking at the right angle," she added.

"What do you mean?" asked Jimmy.

"I mean maybe we should try to find out where he got the spell from."

"That way he won't know we're looking for it, and we'll be able to stop him," said Angela.

"That's actually a very good idea," said Chris.

"Wait, how do we know where to go?" he suddenly asked.

"Wait, didn't you say he got the potion from a witch?" asked Soriya. They all turned and looked at Phillip.

"Yes, he went to this shop, in the town," said Phillip. "I think it was a potion shop, the witch runs it."

"She was walking one day, very pale brown skin with long black hair." "So exactly how are we supposed to get there guys?" asked Jimmy.

"Walking of course!"
shouted Angela.

"It'll be an adventure!"

"I imagine it would only be about ten hours or so." "Ten hours?!" Chris complained.

"How do we even know that for sure?" "She's right," said Phillip. "I followed him here of course and it's true, it's about half a day's travel," he added. "Alright, it's time!" shouted Chris.

"We'll need food, water, anything that won't make this trip as gruesome as it sounds," he added.

"We of course can't be seen by Mr. Hornsbury," said Jimmy. "So we'll leave at night," said Angela.

"But who's to say he won't be sleep?" Chris asked.

"I'll look for you guys," Phillip quickly said. "I'm a ghost, I won't make a sound," he added. "I can get some knapsacks for you all as well."

"Most of the students don't use theirs, so they won't know that some are missing." "Well, let's get ready!" shouted Chris as he grabbed his hands together.

Chris's behavior started to become a little strange to Jimmy. He was very adventurous indeed, but Jimmy found it at times to be too adventurous. Also, a slight sinister smile started to appear whenever adventure called. However, Jimmy brushed it off. "Maybe he just likes adventure," he thought to himself.

"Can we leave in a couple of hours?" asked Soriya.

"I need to go back home and get some things," she added. "Sure," said Chris.

"But we must move quickly. Time isn't on our side." "Ok, I'll be back guys," Soriya said quickly. "Just meet back here?" she asked.

"Meet us back at my house," Chris replied.

"But we can't be seen, he may see us and suspect something. Just try to be discreet," he added.
"Well of course," replied Soriya. "Relax Chris."
"It's not like he's even seen me." "You're acting too paranoid," she added.
"How do you know he hasn't seen you?" Chris asked, in a serious tone. "He could have spies."
"Oh Chris," Soriya laughed. "Sometimes I wonder."

Jimmy looked at Chris's reaction to Soriya statement, and he looked enraged. "Just be back soon please, we have to go," said Chris.
"Okay okay, see you guys soon," said Soriya. "Chris, is everything okay?" asked Jimmy.

"You seem upset."

"I'm fine, we just don't know what we're up against, and I'm worried about my pa," said Chris.
"What if he starts killing people?"

"I don't think that's his plan," assured Jimmy. `

"And besides, we have a couple of days to stop him before the concert." "But we must stay calm, we have to stick together, so that we can stop him," added Jimmy.
"Yes, I know," said Chris.

"Come on, let's get ready," said Chris, as he put his arm around Jimmy.

The teens immediately started packing goods for their trip.
They found containers to temporarily put the supplies in.
They tried to do it discreetly, so they could not be heard.

The Music Man was seated on the couch reading the daily
newspaper, smoking a pipe.
The smoke smelled of oak and cherry.
 "Sir?" asked Jimmy.
"Have you all figured out what you're going to do?" the Music Man
asked. "Well, we are going to Chris's house to try to find tools to
stop Hornsbury," replied Jimmy.
"Tools?" the Music Man asked.
Jimmy nodded his head quickly.
The teens kept looking at each other and the Music Man became
suspicious.
He looked at Jimmy and Angela immediately changed the subject.
"Well, we better get going," she stated, as she started motioning
the group to follow her.
"We have no time to waste if we want to stop Hornsbury."
    "Wait now," the Music Man quickly stated.
    "What are you all really up to?" he asked, looking at the
containers the group had filled.
    "Nothing, we're literally going back to my house," Chris spoke
up.
    "We think we know of a spell that can help stop Hornsbury and
these supplies can help."
    "In fact, my father should be arriving any minute," he added, as
he looked up at the clock that was stationed on the wall.
    Angela started backing up.
    "See you soon Mr. Cornelius!" Jimmy shouted.

The teens immediately followed Angela and quickly shut the door.

The Music Man just stood there, shocked at their abrupt exit.

Chapter 12

Soriya entered her room and began to look for a locket that her grandmother gave her. She opened her dresser drawer and there it was, tucked inside, under her clothes.
She opened it, and there was a picture of her and her grandmother. Her grandmother passed away when she was little. However, she remembered how loving she was. She always gave Soriya sweets and sang to her whenever she was scared or sad. Soriya wanted her locket close to her, for she thought that the locket would serve as good luck and that it coming from her grandmother, was blessed. She kissed it and said, "Love you and miss you grandma."

Soriya shed a tear and then she felt peaceful. She got up and quickly packed some clothes and her hair accessories. Then suddenly, she heard a knock and the door opened.
"Young lady, where do you think you're going?"

Her mom appeared in the doorway, arms folded across her chest.
"Umm, just going to Angela's."
"Well, were you going to ask permission first?" asked her mom, in a serious tone. "Well, I didn't think you or dad were home."
"I didn't see the car," she added.

"It's in the garage dear," said her mother.

"You can go but make sure you come back by tomorrow night, your cousin will be visiting. She's excited to see you," she added.
"Yes ma'am," said Soriya as she smiled. "Well come give me a hug," said her mom.
As they hugged each other, her mom said, "I love you Soriya and I want you to be very happy, you can always talk to me if something is troubling you, okay?" Soriya nodded and smiled at her.
"Mother, what would you do if someone you hardly know is trying to harm others through deceit?" she asked.
"Would you try to stop them?"

"Why of course, especially if I know the people who may be harmed," her mother replied.
"Why? Do you know of such a person?"

Soriya's mother looked deeply into Soriya's eyes. Soriya knew her mother wouldn't believe her, so she lied.
"Well, it's a boy in my orchestra, he's talking to Angela and another girl," she said. "Oh honey, love is a complicated thing, besides you all are very young."
"Trust me, you will have many loves throughout life, you and Angela both. You both are very beautiful, Angela will be okay," said her mom as she smiled.
"I love you mother," Soriya said as she hugged her mother.

She felt a little bad for lying to her but she felt that it was for the greater good. "Okay dear, you run off now. See you tomorrow," said her mom as she kissed Soriya on the cheek.

Her mom left the room and suddenly Soriya began to cry. She felt so bad for lying to her mother but she knew that her mother wouldn't understand. She then got the idea to write her mom a note telling her where she was really going. She placed the note in her dresser, underneath her clothes and shed another tear. Even if her mother were to never find the note, she was still relieved that she at least wrote the truth. She then stood up and composed herself.

At last, she was on her way to the others.

Chapter 13

Phillip went off to gather knapsacks as he promised.

Soriya met back up with the group at Chris's house. Mr. Mcclain wasn't home yet so they made sure to move quickly. The five teenagers then started their journey to the other town, not knowing what to expect along the way.

They made sure to pack flashlights so that they could see. "Well Phillip, after you."

"You know the way," said Soriya, as she pulled out her flashlight.

The Music Man kept looking at the clock, wondering why Jimmy had not returned yet.

He then made his way out of the house in search for Chris's father. As he entered the town square, he spotted the butcher's shop.

"Hello, how may I help you Cornelius?" asked the butcher.

The butcher stood about five feet and eight inches tall. He had red skin with green specks on him.
"Do you know where I can find Mr. McClain?" the Music Man asked the butcher. "Why yes sir, remember he lives over there on the farm," the butcher replied. "Oh."
"Yes of course," said the Music Man. "I will be going now."
"Thank you so much."

"Would you like some meats sir?" asked the butcher. "No thank you, have a good day," replied the Music Man.
As the Music Man made his way to the farm, he bumped into Hornsbury. "My my if it isn't Cornelius," sneered Hornsbury.
"I don't want any trouble," said the Music Man. "Who said anything about trouble?" Hornsbury asked.
"Are you coming to my concert?" "You know…"
"Support a fellow conductor like yourself?" "I definitely will," the Music Man answered. "But I have to get going."
"It will be the concert of your life," sneered Hornsbury.

"Hope to see you there."

Hornsbury chuckled and walked the other way.

The Music Man brushed off Hornsbury and just kept walking. He spotted the farm that William owned.
It was the largest farm in the town.

The Music Man knocked on William's door.

William opened and of course, he had coffee in his hand. "Why Cornelius,"
"What brings you out this way?"

"I'm so happy about the performance." "They did such a good job."
"Would you like some coffee?" "I made some stew."
"Why thank you William," the Music Man responded.

"Is Jimmy here?" he asked.
"No, is he supposed to be?" Mr. Mcclain asked, as he looked around.
The Music Man sighed.

"I think he, your son, and a few others went off to try to stop Hornsbury."
"Off?" William asked.
"Off where?"

"That's just it," the Music Man replied.
"They said they were coming here."

    Suddenly, William became very angry.

"Wait, why would you just let them go?!" shouted Mr. McClain.
"You didn't think to stop them?!"

"I did not think they would actually run off," the Music Man said in a low voice.

"If anything happens to my son, I will hold you personally responsible," said Mr. McClain as he pointed at him.

"Yes."

"I know," said the Music Man.

"Please leave," Mr. Mcclain demanded.

"I am going to pray that nothing happens to him." "He's all I have." "Who knows where they have gone."

"Very well," said the Music Man, in a sad voice. "Again, my apologies sir."

"Leave," Mr. Mcclain said as he held the door open.

The Music Man was upset and shook his head.

He then had an idea to go to Olivia's house to see if she could help him find the teens.

He knocked on her door and she answered of course.

"Yes Cornelius?"

"Is everything okay?"

"Well Jimmy and the others have left and I don't know where they went," the Music Man replied.

"Well I'm sure they'll be back," Olivia replied.

"That's just it, it's getting dark," he responded.

Suddenly, Olivia started to sing again but this time the Music Man couldn't make out the words. It's almost like she was singing in another language.

He started to go into another trance.

Olivia sang for about a minute.

Then she stopped.

"Just calm down Cornelius," she whispered.

"They'll be okay."

The Music Man then nodded his head.

Olivia smiled.

"See you tomorrow?" she asked.

The Music Man nodded his head again and Olivia immediately shut the door.

He was now under a full trance and he quickly made his way back home.

Chapter 14

Soriya thought about the conversation that took place between her and her mother earlier. She knew her mother loved her very much, but they were never really close. Both of her parents worked and her grandmother basically took care of her until she died.

"Jimmy, what was your mother like?" Soriya asked.

Caught off guard and unsure of what to say, since his mother is technically still alive, he responded,

"Well, she was very young but very wise. She taught me to always work hard and to always be humble."

"I miss her every day, she was very beautiful." "I'm sure she was, how did she pass?" Soriya replied.

"If I may ask."

Even more disturbed at the conversation, Jimmy said, "Well, she got ill and died within days."
"Do you know how she got ill? You must've been petrified," she asked.

At this point, Jimmy didn't know what to say.
"I can't remember, I try to block out those memories. To watch your mother die in front of you, is not something you should want to see."
"I understand, well you're a sweet boy, nicer than the other boys I know." Soriya smiled at Jimmy and he smiled back. He thought Soriya was really pretty and very smart for her age. He had never really had a crush before, at least that he could remember. He was always doing chores or just simply keeping his own self company.
"How do we know which way to go?" asked Angela. "Phillip is leading us, remember?" said Chris.
"Well how do we know he's really taking us there?" she mumbled.
"He's a ghost, I doubt that he's trying to harm us," Chris snapped back. "Besides, he wants revenge, so I'm sure he's on our side."

"Right Phillip?" Chris said while walking by Phillip's side again.

"Believe me, Mr. Hornsbury is evil, he needs to be stopped. Look at what he's capable of," said Phillip, referring to himself.
"I don't think he'd spare anyone."

Suddenly, Angela spotted a shadow on one the trees. "Guys look!" she shouted.
Jimmy pointed his flashlight.

"Did you guys see that?" Angela whispered. "See what?" asked Jimmy.
"I saw a shadow of a short figure," Angela responded. Suddenly, a dwarf appeared before them.
"Where are you guys going?" the dwarf asked. "You guys shouldn't be out here."
"Aren't you Harmonians?" "Don't answer him," said Chris.
"You all don't know what's out here," said the dwarf, as he looked around. "You shouldn't be here."
"We are just going somewhere that's very important," said Angela.
"Well, I'm telling you it is dangerous," urged the dwarf.
"Go back, you all are too young to be traveling by yourselves."
"Who are you?" the dwarf asked, as he pointed at Phillip.

"Long story," Phillip said in a low voice, as he looked down.

"Sir, it was nice meeting you, but we are leaving now, thank you," said Chris. "Just be careful," said the dwarf.

The dwarf quickly ran back into the woods, as the others just stared.
"Okay we've been walking for several hours," said Angela.
"We need to rest somewhere and make a fire."

"Do you know anything about these woods Phillip?" "I THINK we'll be okay," answered Phillip.

"Well come on guys, we're wasting time," said Chris, as he led them into a clearing.

The teens pointed their flashlights to make sure they could see everything. "There's a good spot!" shouted Angela.

"Shhh!" said Soriya.

"We can't be too loud, you heard the dwarf." "We don't know what's out here."

"Let's just make a fire and get some rest," said Jimmy as he sat down and rubbed two sticks together.

"How do you know how to do that?" inquired Soriya. "Well, I play outside a lot," answered Jimmy.

"I just know," he added.

"Well good job!" Soriya whispered.

The teens then finished making a fire, laid out blankets, and rested.

The next morning, Soriya woke up and heard birds chirping, as she looked around.

Phillip was just laying there, with his back turned. She couldn't tell whether or not he was sleeping. "Guys!" she shouted.

No one moved. "Guys!"

"We need to get going," she said, as she nudged Jimmy. Jimmy rose up and looked around.

He couldn't believe that he was still there.

The rest of the teens got up and gathered their things. "Come on, we have a ways to go," said Phillip.

The group kept walking for miles with nothing but nature in sight.
Jimmy started to move his fingers, pretending he was playing the piano.
Soriya looked at him and smiled.
She then acted as if she were playing the violin.
Angela looked at them and rolled her eyes.
"Why don't you two just kiss already," she blurted.
Soriya giggled and playfully pushed Angela

The group soon approached a spring.
"Yes!"
"Can't get enough water!" shouted Soriya. She pulled out a canteen and filled it up.
"There may not be water for miles." "Get some water guys!"

Suddenly Jimmy felt a splash on him, and sure enough it was Soriya. "Oops!" she giggled.
Jimmy splashed some water back on her. And next thing, they were engaged in a water fight. Angela then joined, telling Chris to join as well, but as she looked at him, she couldn't speak. Chris's face was expressionless. He just stared at them. This made Angela very uneasy.
"Hey guys, we should stop and keep going." Angela watched Chris as he started to walk again. "Jimmy, how well do you know Chris?"
asked Angela.

"Well, he's the first friend I've made, since I've moved to the town," Jimmy replied.
"Why?"

"Just asking," Angela responded.

Angela really didn't know Chris, as Chris was homeschooled most of the time. In fact, not many of the teens in Harmony Town went to school.
Most of them were homeschooled.

Angela paused and looked to the left.
There was an apple tree standing tall.
"Well I'm hungry!" shouted Angela as she ran to pick one.
"Wait!" "Do you see any other trees around?" asked Jimmy.
"What can possibly be wrong with them?" asked Angela.
"Well, we're walking and haven't crossed anyone else's path, so who planted it?" asked Jimmy.
"Oh stop, I'm sure it's fine," Angela said with a laugh.
"Maybe we should listen to him," suggested Soriya.
"He does have a point."
Suddenly Chris walked up to the tree, "Since you two are scared, I will have two for you."
"Would you like one Phillip?" Chris asked.

"Well, I would have one...if I wasn't a ghost," said Phillip, as he looked down. "Well, I'm sure the apples are fine," Chris said.
"Come on guys, let's go...before it gets dark." And sure enough, the teens followed his lead.

"When does the sun set guys?" asked Soriya.
 "Probably in two hours." said Jimmy.

"Oh wow, have you been counting this entire time?" asked Soriya.
"Well, kind of...I've been keeping track in my head," replied
Jimmy. "Which means, he doesn't know for sure," said Chris.
"Hey, what's your problem?" asked Jimmy.

"Nothing, no one knows the answer to her question. And to be
honest, it doesn't matter anyway, because we can't rest," replied
Chris.
"Time is not on our side."

"Why are you in such a hurry to stop Mr. Hornsbury?" asked
Angela, while giving a side glance to Jimmy.
"Well, let's see, he has killed our good friend Phillip here, has
possessed one town, and is now planning to possess another
town."
"So, I think he should be stopped." "Don't you agree Jimmy?"
"Well of course, but you've been acting strange," said Jimmy.
"That's all," he added.
"How so?" asked Chris.

"You're just getting mad easily, and you seem really angry," said
Jimmy.

"Well, Phillip is our friend, and it is cruel...cruel what happened to
him," Chris replied strongly.

"He's right" Phillip whispered.

So, Chris, how old are you again?" asked Soriya, quickly changing the subject. "Will turn 14 this winter," replied Chris, as he stepped on a pile of leaves. Winter was soon approaching. The beginning fall months allowed for a smooth journey, with no snow.

The weather was always pretty much nice in Harmony Town but in the other towns, they received all the seasons.

"And you Jimmy?" asked Soriya.

"I'm 13 as well, won't turn 14 until next spring."

Jimmy couldn't remember the last time he had a birthday party. With his mom working all the time, he barely cared for his them. Besides, Jimmy didn't have friends. "Why?"

"Are you a birthday planner?" joked Jimmy. "Well, I do love cake," Soriya answered.

"But since we've become friends, we should throw a birthday celebration after our journey," she added.

Followed by no response from the others,

"Or we can just throw a celebration for stopping Hornsbury."

"We haven't stopped him yet," Angela said sharply.

"But we will," Chris said in a loud tone.

"He will NOT get away with what he has done!" he shouted.

With the others staring at him, "Now let's hurry, we don't have much more time."

Angela kneeled down and took her shoes off.

"Guys I am getting blisters."

"Well, there will be much more than blisters if we don't stop him," snapped Chris. Angela quickly rubbed her feet and put her shoes back on.

The teenagers moved at a fast pace, as they felt that they were very close to their destination.

"It's getting dark again," said Soriya as she pulled the flashlight out of her knapsack.

The other teenagers also pulled out their flashlights. "What was that?!" whispered Angela.

"What was what?" asked Jimmy. "I heard a branch snap."

Angela pointed her flashlight to the trees. There was nothing there. "I know I heard something."

Angela kept moving her flashlight amongst the trees. "Come on guys, we have to stay focused," said Jimmy. "I hope no one is following us," Angela said out loud.

"It could just be an animal Angela," suggested Soriya.

Angela sighed.

"I sure hope so."

Angela looked at Soriya and they continued towards their destination.

Chapter 15

"Look guys, I see a tower," pointed Jimmy. The teenagers were quickly approaching the town.

Soriya gulped, "So this is it?"

"Do you think she'll look scary?" she asked. "Who?" asked Angela.

"The witch!" Soriya screamed in an annoyed voice. "Why of course."

"She's a witch," answered Angela.

"So what's the plan?" Angela asked, as she looked at Chris.

"Well, I think it would be smart for one of you to start talking to her, that way she's not intimidated," said Chris.

"And what about Phillip?" Soriya asked, sounding concerned.

"Don't worry about me guys, I want to go check on my family, I can meet back with you all at a specific time," Phillip stated.

"What if someone sees you Phillip?" Jimmy asked. "They won't, it's almost dark," Phillip responded.

Indeed, the sun was setting and Phillip would barely be noticed, nothing more than a resemblance of a shadow.

"We don't have much time, let's go!" screamed Chris, as he started to run.

The teenagers ran to a bench that was empty. It was almost dark and there weren't that many people walking about.

"Don't worry guys, there isn't much of a crowd at this time, except for the police. They're the ones you have to watch out for. They'll ask what we're doing.

I remember one time, my friends and I were just hanging out by the abandoned theater, and they thought we were up to something. So we must not appear like "We're up to something," said Phillip.

"Do you think that they know who isn't part of this town?" asked Soriya. "No, but if we look suspicious, they'll come around," answered Phillip.

Jimmy was looking around for another area that was hidden for them to meet back at.

"How about over there?" Jimmy asked, as he pointed. "Near the park?" he added.

"Hmm that's a good spot," said Phillip.

"But we must leave right when it's dark, just in case there are people still walking. If someone is shocked by our presence, then that will create a commotion," said Phillip.

"Well, let's not waste any more time then, come on!" shouted Chris. "So Phillip, you're going to look for your family right?" asked Chris. "Do you remember where they live?"

"I don't think they would move, but yes, I do," said Phillip.

"Specifically where should I meet you guys at?" he also asked.

"Let's meet at the bench," answered Chris.

"But wait, won't the witch be with us?" asked Angela with a confused look on her face.

"Yes, and I think that's a good idea, because she'll see Phillip as a ghost, so that she knows we're not lying," said Chris.

"Yes, that's a good idea Chris," said Angela. "Okay, see you Phillip," said Chris.

"Wait, what time shall we meet back here?" Phillip asked.

"I would imagine it shouldn't take more than a hour," said Soriya.

"Yes, a hour should be good," said Phillip.

"Besides, her house is just beyond the graveyard,"
he added, as he pointed in that direction.

"Is it just me or does anyone else have a weird feeling about
this?" asked Angela, as she gulped.
"It's just a graveyard guys, we didn't come all this way for nothing,
we don't have much time."
"Let's move!" shouted Chris.

"What is your problem?" shouted Soriya.

"You have been acting so strange since the first time Angela and I
met you," she added.
"I have already explained, I am upset okay?" "This is very
serious."
"But still, you can calm down a little bit," said Soriya. "Wait guys,
isn't this town possessed?" asked Jimmy. "Short answer, yes,"
Phillip responded.
"Long answer, not all," he added. "What do you mean?" asked
Jimmy.
"Not everyone went to his concert," said Phillip.

"So, if someone who is possessed sees us?" asked Angela.

"I don't know what will happen, but I do know that there's no way
for them to tell Hornsbury where we are," Phillip replied.

"Great, we don't know what to expect, how awesome," said
Angela. "Let's just keep to the plan, see you in a hour Phillip,"
said Chris.

"Be careful guys, and remember, don't appear suspicious," said Phillip as he wandered off.

"How can we not appear suspicious if there aren't that many people out?" asked Angela.

Jimmy stood up and looked around.

"Well, there are some people, even teenagers!" Jimmy shouted. "Look."

"Over there," he pointed.

There indeed were teenagers just standing around. "Look! There are also Harmonians!" shouted Soriya. "See, we should blend in easily," Chris said confidently. "Come on, let's go!" Chris ordered. "There's the graveyard."

"No one get fidgety," he added.

The four of them gathered behind each other, with Chris taking the lead. "You guys lost?" asked one of the teens that Jimmy spotted.

The teenagers looked normal, like the world where Jimmy was originally from. However, their eyes were fixated, and had a strange look to them. "No, thanks," said Chris.

Angela looked back at Soriya in a worried manner.

"You guys aren't from here," said the boy.

The teenagers looked like they were almost 18.

There were three boys and one girl. All of them were smoking cigarettes. "We are, thanks," said Chris.

He was trying to keep the conversation short but the boy just kept asking questions. Soriya reached out for Jimmy's hand, and whispered in his ear.

"I think they're possessed," she whispered. "How do you know?" he whispered back. "I just have a feeling."

"Besides, look at their eyes."

"Hey, your jacket is pretty, where'd you get it?" asked the girl, as she was looking at Angela.

"My grand mom got it for me, she's expecting me back," said Angela quickly. "What's your grand mom's name?"

"Maybe I know her," the girl also asked. Chris was getting frustrated at this point.

"Look guys, we don't want any trouble, we have to be in by a certain time, have a great evening," said Chris.

Angela was surprised at the tone of Chris's voice, he sounded so mature and the frustration in his voice could be heard.

"Yikes, okay, well take care," said the teen boy, with his hands up mimicking a surrender.

"Oh, hope you're not heading up to the graveyard." "It's haunted." The rest of the teenagers laughed. "And the witch…"

"Well, you'll find out when you meet her," the teen smirked, as he winked at them.

"Come on guys, let's just stay focused," Chris said, as the others followed him.

Soriya was very scared, and looked back at the teens. They all just stared at her with a blank stare.

"Chris, how could they have known where we're going?" she asked.

"They're probably possessed, and maybe they know the witch has the spells," said Chris.

"I have such a bad feeling about this Chris, it just doesn't add up," said Soriya. "What did you expect?"

"For us to just walk up to her with ease and ask for the spell?"

"She gave it to him Soriya, use your head," responded Chris.

"I'm sure they made some kind of pact, agreement, something," he added. "Come on."

"Let's go," instructed Chris.

Jimmy put his arm around Soriya, and whispered in her ear, "It will be okay, I'll protect you."

At that moment, Soriya knew that Jimmy cared for her.

"Guys, what are they doing!?" stuttered Angela, as she was looking at the graveyard.

"Oh my!" shrieked Soriya, as she covered her mouth. There were little kids, standing around a grave, looking down. At this point, Chris was fed up and shouted at Angela.

"Stop being distracted, you heard that boy, he said it's haunted Angela, which probably means IT'S HAUNTED!"

"I'll just go to the witch myself, I'll find you guys later," said Chris, as he started to walk off.

"Jimmy," Chris continued to say as he looked at Soriya and Angela. "Good luck."

"We should've just came by ourselves." "You're such a jerk!" shouted Angela.

Chris ignored her statement and walked off to the witch's house.

"Come on guys, let's just try to find the potion shop," said Jimmy, as he started to walk the other way.

Angela stood there, grimacing, and then she decided to follow Jimmy. Soriya just simply shook her head, sighed, and followed as well.

Chris didn't know what his plan was but he knew he had to get the spell book. He started to take deep breaths and looked around in the graveyard to see if anyone was looking. He noticed that the group of kids disappeared. He trembled and took

a deep breath.

He then knocked on the witch's door, nervously. Suddenly, a light flickered on and off in the witch's house. He took a step back and the door slowly opened. "I am guessing you are Chris?" the witch asked very slowly. She was very lanky, with long black hair and a very skeletal voice. Her skin was brown with a sly look on her face. Chris was frightened at the sight of her. "How, how did you know that?" he asked as he gulped. "My dear, I am a witch, and

also psychic." "And you want my book, but you're not going to get it."
"It's not here."

"You're not the first to come to try to take it from me," she added.

"You don't know what you're doing, the man you gave one of your spells to is trying to possess my town," pleaded Chris.
"Well, surely we made a deal, and surely I won't break that deal," the witch responded, as she poked at the fireplace. "I was just making a pot of tea."

"Come, sit down, you must be cold," she said as she smiled at him. "I am fine, I don't want your book, I just want the spell," said Chris. "No, do not ask again," the witch snapped back.
"Besides, why should I give it to you?" she asked. "To stop him!" Chris shouted.
"But you!" the witch screamed and all of a sudden Chris picked up a poker from the fireplace and stabbed the witch in the eye.
The witch fell down, and hit her head against the floor. She then gasped and her eyes were fastly shut.

Chris looked around, looking for something to tie her hands with. He figured that she would be unconscious for a while so he figured he would try to look for her spell book. He went into another room, and he was taken aback by how many cats she had. There were black curtains and a strange scent coming from another room. He was unsure as to whether or not he would want to find what was in there. He shrieked in horror, as a cat was just standing on the table, staring at him. And surrounding the cat was a symbol drawn in black ink. Chris quickly shut the door, not sure where to look next for the book. Suddenly, he remembered the graveyard. He walked outside and looked at the graves. The grave that the children surrounded had a strange gravestone with markings on it. The gravestone read "R.I.P Lenora". Not knowing who Lenora was, he decided to dig the grave up, and sure enough, the spell book was there. "She named the grave stone Lenora to make people think that a person was buried there," Chris said to himself.

Chris smiled really wide at the thought that he now possessed the infamous spell book. "Now, to get rid of you," Chris said as he looked back at the witch's house. He wrapped the frail witch in a sheet so that no one could see her. It was very dark, so he figured no one would be outside.

He drug her body across the graveyard to the grave marked Lenora and pushed her into it.

Not waiting another second, he dumped and dumped the dirt on her. The grave was only four feet deep but he was sure that it was deep enough. "You were wrong and I now have your book!" Chris shouted as he looked at the book. He thought to himself that the others couldn't find out what he had done. "They wouldn't understand."

Chris turned page after page, not knowing where the specific spell was. "It has to be somewhere!" he shouted.

He looked at the witch, who lay unconsciously in the grave. "Think, think," he said to himself.

He stood there for five minutes, rummaging through the pages, as he kept glancing at the witch, making sure she didn't awake. "Yes!" shouted Chris.

And there it was, the spell. Chris knew it was the spell, because on the bottom of the page was signed Jubilee Hornsbury's name.
"Make it known Truth be told
The one who possesses this spell
Their soul they will sell
For power of them all
Comes at a price
You must think twice.
Now if you want to,
Then continue...
Drink the potion

And you will have power

To do anything your heart desires."

On the next page, the reversal spell displayed,
"If you want the former stopped
Then you must do these things
Destroy the potion
For it adds power
   Give it time
   And you will see
   The person who bought this spell from me
Will no longer be."
"Also, you must say this spell out loud five times."

Chris ripped the reversal spell out of the book, put it in his pocket, slammed the book shut, and tossed it back into the grave.

Chapter 16

Phillip stood outside the window of his parent's home. Everything was as it was. Only there was something that made him shed a tear. His baby brother had grew. There his family was, sitting in the living room, smiling, happy. What happened next surprised Phillip, as his mother looked directly at him.
Suddenly, she screamed with her hand over her face. His father looked up and the baby started to cry. And before they knew it, Phillip disappeared.

"There he is!" shouted Soriya, as she pointed at Phillip.

"Oh no, he's crying," Angela stated with concern.

"Come on," said Jimmy as he started to run to catch up with him.
"What happened?" Jimmy asked.
"I saw my family, and they saw me," Phillip cried.
"Oh wow," said Soriya.
"Well, do you want to go back? So they know what happened?"
"No! I don't want them to see me like this."
"They're happy with my baby brother anyway, they forgot about me!" shouted Phillip, as he kicked a fence.
"No, Phillip, they didn't," said Soriya in a soft tone.

"How would you know?" he asked.

"Because, I lost my sister two years ago, and my mom couldn't take it. My parents wanted another child, to ease the pain," she said.

"What happened to her?" asked Phillip.

"She drowned and she didn't come back, so don't be mad at them and she probably screamed because she's in shock that you're here."

"But I'm not here, I'm not the same," Phillip said.

"Still, Phillip, I am sure your parents miss you very much. You should go back," said Angela.

"I don't want to make my mom sad," Phillip replied.

"I doubt she will be sad, let's just go back there okay?" asked Jimmy.

"We'll go there with you," he added.

Phillip looked up, and all three faces were staring at him, with genuine care. "Okay," he said.

Jimmy wrapped his arm around Phillip.

Even though, his arm went through him, Phillip appreciated the gesture. "Where's Chris?" Phillip asked, noticing Chris wasn't there.

"He went to the witch's house by himself," responded Jimmy.

"We were trying to look for the potion shop but then we saw you."

"It's not that far from here," said Phillip.

"Hopefully Chris has some luck at her house," he added. "Come on, let's go to your house,"

Jimmy instructed.
Phillip nodded and lead the way.

"This is it," said Phillip as he pointed at his house.
 "Here goes nothing," said Jimmy, as he took a deep breath and knocked on the door. The teenagers waited for about a minute with no response.
"Do you think they're still there?" asked Jimmy.

"Where else would they have gone? It's almost midnight," said Soriya.
Just as Jimmy proceeded to knock again, a low voice answered.
"Who is it?"

"I think that's my father," said Phillip.

"Hello sir, sorry to disturb you, but your son is outside, with his friends," said Jimmy.
"I only have one son and he's here with me," the voice said loudly.
"Now go away before I call the police!" he shouted.
Suddenly, a sweet voice followed, and said,

"You will do no such thing, and yes, we did have a son."

Phillip looked up, hoping with all of his heart, that his mom would open the door. And sure enough, the door opened slowly.
His father had gone to sit on the sofa, with his face buried in a pillow. Phillip's father was tall with ivory skin, and was very handsome.
 "Phillip?" his mother asked him, trying not to scream.

Phillip's mother had ivory skin with long brown hair. She was shorter in statue, with pretty brown eyes.

"It's me mom," Phillip said.

"Oh my son!" she said as she took him in her arms. "What happened to you?"
"You're a ghost."

"My music conductor put a very powerful spell on me," he answered. Suddenly, Phillip's father looked up with a very strange look in his eyes.
"We thought you had ran away," his father said.
"We must find him, he can't get away with this," he added.
"No father, we are going to handle it," said Phillip.
"You believe that I am a ghost, so you will believe me when I tell you this."

"He wants to possess my friends' entire town, he's possessed a lot here already," said Phillip.
"Have you noticed anyone acting strange?" he added. "All of the time," responded Phillip's mother.
 "Almost everyone," she added.
"You all didn't go to my concert did you?" asked Phillip.
"No, we were too busy looking for you," his dad answered.
"That's how he did it, the people who attended; he possessed them through his music," said Phillip.
"The town's witch gave him a potion and a spell," he added.

"And we're going to stop him," interjected Jimmy. All three teenagers introduced themselves.

"I'm Soriya."

"I'm Angela."

"I am Jimmy."

"He will not get away with murdering your son," said Jimmy, in a mature and confident manner.

Suddenly, the baby started to cry.

"May I hold him?" asked Soriya.

"Why of course you can," Phillip's mother replied.

"He is so precious," Soriya said, smiling at him.

She picked him up and rocked him in her arms.

"Uh oh, what time is it?" asked Angela, as she turned and looked at Jimmy.

"It is 30 minutes past midnight," said Phillip's father.

"Chris!" Soriya and Angela both shouted at the same time.

The baby started to cry again and Soriya put him back into his crib.

"I'm sorry little one," Soriya whispered.

"We have to go help your big brother," she added.

Jimmy was still talking to Phillip's mother and Soriya walked up to the rest of the group.

"It was nice meeting you both, but we really have to go," said Soriya, as she pulled Jimmy towards her.

Jimmy quickly got the message and followed Soriya's lead.

"Phillip, you can stay if you want," said Jimmy.

"We'll come back for you," he added. "Thanks guys," smiled Phillip.

Although it was strange hugging a ghost, Phillip's parents warmly embraced him. Jimmy turned to look back at Phillip, however Phillip was too consumed with the affection of his parents.

As the door of Phillip's parents slammed shut, Angela asked, "What do you think has happened with Chris?"
"I hope he's not lost or even worse, has left us!"
"I don't think so," said Jimmy.
"He's really not that bad Angela."

"Well his outbursts sure are proving you wrong," she replied.
"Come on guys, we need to focus," said Soriya.
"Where is the graveyard?" she asked.
"I think it's back that way," answered Jimmy.

"I thought Chris said to meet him back at the bench at midnight?" asked Angela.
        The teens all turned to look at each other, unsure of what to do.
"Okay, let's think," said Soriya.
"Jimmy, you know him best," she said. "Where do you think he is?"
"Let's just go to the bench," replied Jimmy.

"Besides, remember the graveyard isn't that much further from the town square."
"You're right! Good memory Jimmy," Soriya said, as she smiled at him.

114

"Come on you two, we don't have much time. You can kiss when we kill Hornsbury," Angela said.

Immediately Angela paused, taken aback by the word "kill". She couldn't believe it came out of her mouth. Could she really kill someone, someone stronger than her for that matter? She exhaled and shook the thought off. It's all for the greater good, she thought in her head.

Jimmy was right; Chris was indeed sitting at the bench.

"Did she give you the spell?" asked Angela, wasting no time, walking up to Chris.
"What was she like?"
"Were you scared?"
"So many questions Angela, I told you I would get the spell from her," replied Chris.

"What happened?" asked Jimmy.
"Well, it happened really fast."
"I simply knocked on the door, she answered. I then told her who I was and what I needed. You know, got straight to the point. She was very scared for us and immediately gave me the spell," said Chris.
Soriya looked at Angela and saw that she had a suspicious look on her face. "So, what's the spell?" asked Jimmy.
"It's an easy chant, have it here in my pocket," said Chris.

"But we have to get back guys, now that we have what we needed."

"Oh no, I'm not going anywhere, it's dark," said Angela.

"Fine, we'll sleep in the park but we must leave immediately when the sun rises," said Chris.

"I have an idea; let's just go back to Phillip's house," suggested Soriya.

"That way, we will be warm and no one will question why we're laying on the ground outside," she added.

"Good thinking!" shouted Angela.

"Where is Phillip by the way?" asked Chris.

"He decided to stay with his parents," replied Jimmy.

"Well let's go to their house," said Chris.

The rest of the group nodded their heads and began walking to Phillip's house, with Jimmy leading the way.

Chapter 17

A slow and steady knock was heard at the door.

"Hello again, we were wondering if we could sleep here for the night," asked Soriya, in a soft voice.

"I don't think that would be a problem dear," answered Phillip's mother.

"We have extra rooms upstairs, but you all must be cold."

"Would you like some tea and cake?"

"Come sit by the fire, Phillip's sound a sleep," she added.

"I didn't know ghosts slept," whispered Angela to Soriya.

Phillip's mother heard Angela's comment.
 "Why wouldn't they?" asked Phillip's mother. Shocked that she was heard,
"I just thought that since they are already dead, that they don't need sleep," replied Angela.
"Maybe so, I wouldn't know of course," said Phillip's mother.

"I am just glad to have my Phillip home, we have missed him a great deal." "Who might you be?" she asked, as she looked at Chris.
"I am Chris ma'am, I wasn't here earlier," he said.

Unsure of whether or not to mention the spell to her, he quickly changed the subject.
"You're right, I am freezing."

"I'd like some tea and cake please," he said.

"Well, you all just have a seat at the table and I'll prepare your rooms as well," said Phillip's mother.
"Thank you ma'am," said Soriya.

"Please, call me Mrs. Mosson," said Phillip's mother.

The teenagers never knew Phillip's last name and exchanged glances at each other.

"Where is Mr. Mosson?" asked Soriya.

"Asleep with the baby, he fell asleep shortly before you all knocked on the door as a matter of fact," Mrs. Mosson replied.

Mrs. Mosson proceeded to place cake on the table, handing each of them a warm cup of tea. A pot was already brewed, and the cake was leftovers from yesterday. The teens didn't mind about the cake, as they were very hungry.

"This is delicious," said Chris.

"Calm down, Chris, before you choke," said Angela while laughing. Suddenly, a noise came from the couch.

"He's awake," Mrs. Mosson whispered to them.

"You made it back Chris," Phillip said, with a smile.

"What was she like?"

Chris looked up.

"She was somewhat frightening, but she gave me it," Chris replied.

"She just gave it to you?" asked Phillip.

"Well, not exactly."

"I had to convince her," said Chris.

"Wow, never thought a witch would just hand over a spell," Phillip said.

"A witch?" asked Mrs. Mosson as she looked up.
"What witch?"
"The witch in the town mother," Phillip replied.
"She's the one that gave Mr. Hornsbury the spell."

Mrs. Mosson had a disturbed look on her face.
"I'm going to go check on your father."
"You all eat up now, I'll prepare your rooms as well," she added.

The teens finished their cake and drank their tea, and were ready
for a good night's sleep.
"Okay you all, come along," said Phillip's mother, as she walked
back in the kitchen.
"Angela and Soriya,"

"You two can sleep in this room."
"And Jimmy and Chris,"
"You can sleep in this room."

Both of the spare rooms were downstairs.
    The house was very beautiful, and each of the spare rooms
had a couch and a bed.
"I'm taking the bed!" shouted Angela, as she jumped on the bed.
"Ha...ha," laughed Soriya.
"This feels so comfy," said Angela, as she yawned deeply.

"Phillip's mother sure is nice."
    "Yes, the dad seems a little mean though," replied Soriya.
"Yeah, who knows," sighed Angela.

"I'm going to bed."

"Sweet dreams."

"Sweet dreams," yawned Soriya, as she turned over.

"He's not going anywhere," said a whisper in a deep voice. Jimmy had awaken from his sleep because of noises coming from upstairs. "I don't want to lose him again Jonathan," cried Phillip's mother.

"We won't," said his father.

Jimmy looked around, to make sure the others were asleep, especially Phillip. He stood up to stand at the bottom of the stairs. "Those are his friends, you know he'll want to go with them," said Phillip's mother. "I know this, but I promise you I won't let him," assured Phillip's father.

"He's a ghost," replied his mother.

"What are you going to do? Grab him by his hand as he tries to leave?" "Your hand will go right through him."

"Well, what do you suggest I do?" Phillip's father replied.

"Tell him that it's dangerous!" shouted his mother.

"He's already dead. What more can happen to him?" asked Phillip's father.

"I can't believe you just said that," said his mother.

"But he is dead, our boy is not the same as he used to be."

"We have to let him go, eventually."
"We can't live with a ghost forever," said his father.

"I'm finished with this conversation," Mrs. Mosson replied in a very low voice.

Jimmy couldn't make sense of what he just heard. Would Phillip really leave his home to come with them? Could he die again even though he was already dead?
Those were the thoughts that swarmed around in Jimmy's head. Back to bed he went.

Chapter 18

An aroma filled the air and had awakened the teenagers.
"What is that smell?" Jimmy asked out loud.
"Sausages!" he exclaimed in excitement.
Everyone rushed to the table.

"Thank you Mrs. Mosson," said Jimmy in gratitude. "These smell delicious."
"You're welcome dear." Chris awoke as well.
"We really need to be going guys."

"Chris, we can stay awhile, it's only 7 am for Pete's sake" said Angela. "Exactly, which is why we should've left a hour ago," Chris replied.

Angela shook her head in frustration.

"The concert isn't until later tomorrow Chris, lighten up," said Soriya.

"Fine, we'll just act as if everything is going as planned and that maybe just maybe he hasn't rescheduled it to an earlier date," replied Chris.

"Chris, what is your problem?" asked Jimmy.

"We want to stop Hornsbury just as much as you do, but your temper is getting out of hand.".

"You're only saying that to stand up for your girlfriend," Chris said, as he looked at Soriya.

"Hey hey, I'm sure everything will be fine," said Phillips's mother. "Now you all eat your food before it gets cold."

"Besides, you all need to be well fed for your journey back."

Suddenly, Phillip stood up from the sofa.

"Hey sleepy head," Angela giggled.

"I'm glad you guys didn't leave me behind, I've thought of a strategy," said Phillip.

"Son, I think they will have it handled, just stay here with us."

"You don't know how happy we are to have you back here," said his mother.

"I am happy too mother but I can't just desert my friends."

"Besides, I want Hornsbury to pay for what he has done," said Phillip.

"Not a day goes by when I don't go back to that day when he put that spell on me."

"Son, we understand but."

"But what? I'm already dead, there's nothing more he can do to me," said Phillip.
 "Are you sure my son?" Mrs. Mosson asked, as she looked into her son's eyes.
 "You're dealing with magic, how do you know he doesn't have other spells?" his mother asked.
Quickly, Jimmy looked up at Soriya with a worried look on his face.
 "She's right, how do we know that he doesn't have other spells?" asked Soriya.
"Because the witch said so, she didn't mention other spells," replied Chris.
"Chris, that doesn't mean she didn't give him any others," said Soriya. "Trust me, I know," said Chris.
"Look, mother I have to go with my friends. It will be okay," said Phillip.
Mrs. Mosson sighed.
"Okay dear, please be careful, I don't care what your father says. I want my son back home, even if you are a ghost," his mother said in a low voice, looking down.
"We are going to try to reverse the spell Hornsbury put on him," interjected Chris.

"So he can come back."

"You think I can come back to life?" Phillip asked, as his eyes filled with hope.

"We will certainly try," Chris responded.

"Well I sure hope it works," Phillip's mother replied.

"I'll always love you," she cried as a tear rolled down her cheek.

She stood up and wiped the tear from her eye.
"You all be safe."

"Well let's hurry and go so we can get you back in your form," said Chris, as he also rose from the table.
Everyone hugged and thanked Mrs. Mosson for the delicious meal.

Since she couldn't physically hug her son, she just looked at him and smiled.
"Be careful my son, all of you be careful."

As the others were heading out the door, Soriya looked back and Phillip's father was just standing at the top of the stairs. There was no expression, nothing, he just simply stared at them leaving. Suddenly, something behind him moved past him.

Soriya covered her mouth and gasped.

 "Soriya, what are you looking at?" asked Jimmy.

"I just saw something move past Phillip's father," she said as she turned and looked at Jimmy.

"There's no one there," said Jimmy.

And he was right; no one was at the top of the stairs.

"But his father was just right there," said Soriya.

"My dad left for work earlier this morning," said Phillip.

"He didn't say bye, I think he is still in disbelief that I'm back in a form of a ghost."

"Look, we're all tired. Let's just hurry back so that we can stop Hornsbury," Jimmy stated.

"I'll probably be imagining things next," said Angela as she laughed. "Jimmy, I wasn't imagining it. I know what I saw," said Soriya.

"You heard Phillip, his dad left this morning," replied Jimmy.

"Well there's something in there with Phillip's mother and the baby," whispered Soriya.

"Aren't you concerned?" she asked with confusion in her eyes.

"You're probably really tired and with all of this magic happening, it's probably just confusing you," said Jimmy.

"Yeah, I'm sure you're right," said Soriya, as she looked down.

Soriya looked back at the house and then proceeded to look in front of her.

Chapter 19

"So Phillip, how do we get back?" asked Angela.

"We just go back to the center and walk back the way we came," answered Phillip.
"I'll lead the way."
"We're almost there, almost there to kill him," said Chris as he grabbed his fists.
Angela exchanged worried looks with Soriya.
Soriya just shook her head and grabbed Jimmy's hand.

Meanwhile, the Music Man and Olivia were sitting on the couch.

"I really enjoy spending time with you," said Olivia, as she looked into the Music Man's eyes.
"I really enjoy spending time with you too," the Music Man smiled.
"I wonder how the kids are doing," he said.
"I can't believe they left like that."

"Don't worry Cornelius," Olivia smiled.
"They probably went to visit the witch," she added.
"Witch? What witch?" the Music Man, asked in a confused voice.
Olivia giggled.
"She's harmless, she lives in the town that I moved to."

"She just helps people."

The Music Man quickly stood up and decided he would go to the town to find the teens.

 "I'm sure they're just fine Cornelius."

"I know Soriya's mother. That Soriya is a smart girl, they'll be ok," Olivia quickly stated, as she grabbed his hand.

"Besides, if they left a few days ago, they're probably already on their way back now."

"Come sit back down," she smiled.

"But they could be in danger!" the Music Man shouted.

"I doubt it," Olivia smiled.

The Music Man felt hypnotized by Olivia's calmness.

She then started to sing again, in another language.

The Music Man just stood there and stared into her eyes.

He took a deep breath and then sat back down.

"So, how is it that you're not married?" he asked.

"I couldn't imagine any man passing you up."

"My first husband died," Olivia answered.

"How? if you don't mind me asking?" the Music Man asked.

 "He succumbed to an illness, can't remember the name."

"I have made myself forget, too many painful memories."

"I'm sorry," said the Music Man.

"It's okay, you're here now," Olivia smiled.

"Do you still think about her?" asked Olivia, referring to his wife.

 "Well, before I met you,"

"Everyday."

"But now.."

"Not so much."

"You remind me of her in many ways, she was very sweet like you."

"I am happy now, haven't been this happy for a very long time," said the Music Man.
"You and Jimmy have made me a very happy man."
He thought to himself that he would ask Olivia to come back with them when they decided to leave her world.

"Do you ever plan to leave this town?" he asked.

"Haven't thought about it yet, but with you, well yes!" laughed Olivia.
"You know," Olivia started to say.
"It's interesting how this town came about."

"The young boy who traveled here originated from magic. One of the witches created him with a warlock. The witch did a spell that went wrong and it transformed the child in a strange way. He inherited dna and a special pigment. The spell basically changed the pigment of the child's skin to the different blue, purple, and other colors you have seen. That child then traveled to Harmony town and mated with a person living there and then the race arose; Harmonians. Every child after inherited some form of special pigment. The couple vowed that this would be a peaceful town and that magic wouldn't be used. The warlocks and witches in the other towns were killed off, that we know of, but only one witch still exists I believe. She lives in another town.
"Wow, it makes sense now," said the Music Man.

"So, do other towns practice magic?" he asked.

"They're not supposed to," Olivia replied.

"And the witch who supposedly still exists, is protected by a spell her mother casted."

"I hope it's the same witch Jimmy and the teens are visiting."

"If not, another war may break out."

"A war?" asked the Music Man.

"Between who?"

"The witches, people who use magic, and the people who don't," answered Olivia.

"There was a war, supposedly a hundred years back."

"Supposedly all of the witches and warlocks were supposed to have been killed off."

"Dwarves were killed off as well."

"But if another witch does exist, then who knows what else is out there." "It's just scary, you know."

"Well let's not talk about it anymore," said the Music Man.

He then leaned forward and kissed Olivia slowly, enjoying every second.

"I love you," he said.

"I love you too," Olivia smiled, as she blushed.

"You know what I think?" asked Olivia.

"Yes?" asked the Music Man, as he looked into her eyes.

"I think we should go on that picnic now."

"There's a lake not too far from here."

"It has a lot of trees, which is good for shade."

"And the grass is always green, and nicely cut."

"Well, why not?" said the Music Man.

"I love spending time with you, and it sounds fun."
Olivia looked at the Music Man and smiled.
She quickly gave him a hug.

"Let's pack some lunch!" Olivia shouted.

The Music Man laughed and quickly rose to his feet.

"I think some turkey sandwiches will do," he smiled as he looked
in the refrigerator.
"Do you like pickles?" he asked.
"Why, yes I do," said Olivia.
 "Hmm...I don't have any sweets."
"Well, we can certainly stop at the bakery, they have a lot of
cakes and cookies," said Olivia.
"Alrighty, ready?" the Music Man asked, as he reached out his
arm, ready to accompany Olivia.
"Yes, Cornelius," smiled Olivia.

The Music Man and Olivia quickly made their way to the bakery.

As Olivia and the Music Man walked, he suddenly remembered
he would try to warn some people as he promised Jimmy.
The Music Man saw a dwarf and walked up to him.
"Excuse me sir."

"You must not go to Hornsbury's concert tomorrow."
 "Bad things might happen."

"Get out of my way," said the disgruntled dwarf.
"You don't know about bad things."
"This is the most peaceful town."
 "Hornsbury means no harm."
"You just want all the continued fame to go to you."

"No, I am telling you this because it is truth," said the Music Man.
"Come on Cornelius, let's go," said Olivia, as she she took his hand.
"He doesn't want to hear this."

"Well we will see, won't we?" said the dwarf.

The dwarf quickly moved past Cornelius and Olivia.

"Oh and Cornelius, try having most of your entire race killed off."

"Now, that's bad."

Cornelius looked at the dwarf with somber eyes.
"Come on hun," said Olivia.
"Don't worry about him."

"Look! There's the bakery!" she shouted.

The Music Man just stared as the dwarf walked off.

Olivia and the Music Man entered the bakery.
"How may I help you?" asked a lady, who was medium height with short brown hair and pink streaks. Her skin was lavender with red specks.
She wore glasses and had a pleasant look on her face.

"We would just like some cake and a couple of cookies," said Olivia. "Certainly," said the baker.
"You know, you look really familiar," said the baker, as she looked at Olivia. "Well I just moved back here, so maybe you saw me walking about," answered Olivia.
"Hmm, maybe," the baker responded.

The baker packed a couple of slices of cake and cookies for them.
 "Thank you so very much," said Olivia.
The baker started to ask,
"Do you have a brot...?"
"No," Olivia responded very quickly.
"You don't even know what I was going to say," replied the baker.
"I only have a sister, and like I said..."
"I just moved back to this town."

"Well you could try being a little nicer," mumbled the baker.
"Well,"

"I hope you two have a pleasant rest of your day," the baker said sarcastically, as she cashed the two out.
"You have a good day as well," replied Olivia. The baker rolled her eyes.

"Good day miss," said the Music Man.
 "Well. .." he started to say.
"That was odd."
 "Very," said Olivia.
"She probably just saw me walking with my sister."
 "Or has me confused with someone else."
"When do I get to meet your sister by the way?" asked the Music Man. "Soon, my love," Olivia smiled.
The Music Man knew he had to go back to his real town, but he was so in love with Olivia that he lost himself whenever he was around her.
"Lake's over there," said Olivia.

Olivia was right. The grass was very green and freshly cut. The lake was clean, and was as blue as the sky.
It was a perfect sunny day, and the two couldn't be happier.

Olivia laid down a blanket and the two ate and laughed, enjoying each other's company.
The Music Man started to rub Olivia's hands.

He looked deep into her eyes and kissed her on the lips. He hadn't kissed another woman since his wife.

The two then started to feed each other cakes and cookies.

"It's so pretty out here," said Olivia.
"And peaceful."

"Yes, it certainly is."
"I noticed it's always sunny here," said the Music Man.
"Well don't you know?" asked Olivia.
"This is the only town that is pretty much perfect all year round."
"On some occasions, it may rain for an hour or two."
"But that's pretty much it."
 "In the town I moved from,"
"It rained and snowed."
"Is this the only town you've visited outside of your old town?" asked the Music Man.
"Well, we're from this town," said Olivia.

"My mom moved us when we were little, a lot of Harmonians have moved away and a lot have moved back."
"Anyway, my mom got sick and then my sister got tired of living in the other town."
"So she moved back here." "And then I followed."
"What's your sister like?" asked the Music Man.
"She's smart and funny."

"You'll meet her."

"Can't wait!" exclaimed the Music Man.
 "What time is it?" asked Olivia suddenly.
"I don't know," replied the Music Man.

"I don't have my watch."

"We better get going," Olivia said, as she stood up quickly.

The Music Man was taken aback at how suddenly Olivia wanted to leave. "Is everything okay?" asked the Music Man.
"Yes, just have to go meet up with my sister."
The Music Man stood up, with a confused look on his face.
However, he decided not to ask any more questions.
The two then picked up their belongings and hurried off into town.

"We must be ready," Hornsbury said to himself.
He stood in his rehearsal room, in front of the mirror. Suddenly, there was a knock on the door.
"I am busy, who is it?" asked Hornsbury.

The door slowly opened, and there were a set of twins, about 13 years old. Both were boys, with brown hair and brown eyes, and tan skin.
"Sir, are we practicing today?" asked John, one of the twins.
"We practice every day!" shouted Hornsbury.

"We're performing in one day, what kind of question is that?"
"Well sir, it's noon," John responded.
"I know what time it is, do you know what you're supposed to be doing during this time?" Hornsbury asked.
He stared at the boys, waiting for a response.

"Practice! You all should know the piece by heart," shouted Hornsbury. "Well sir, usually you're conducting and Jennifer told us to ask you if practice was still on," said Justin, the other twin. "Jennifer eh? Go tell Jennifer her rations have been taken away for this evening,"

Hornsbury instructed.

"Wait, she has to eat or else she won't be able to play," he said to himself.

"Tell Jennifer that she can conduct for now, she knows how," said Hornsbury. "I will conduct during our evening practice," he added. "Okay sir," said John.

"We are hungry as well," said Justin.

John quickly looked at Justin, afraid that Hornsbury would punish Justin for being hungry.
"Are you now?" asked Hornsbury.

"Have Jennifer make all of you something to eat. I will be in the concert hall a quarter before five," said Hornsbury.

"So tell the others not to bother me before then,"
"Understood?" asked Hornsbury.
"Yes sir," said John and Justin with a nod from each.
"Now, go make some music!" shouted Hornsbury.
"Yes sir," they both replied.

Hornsbury quickly followed them, and as they left, he slammed the door shut. "You would think that I having control over them, that they would follow everything that I tell them to do," sighed Hornsbury.

He cast a spell on his students which took away their ability to think for

themselves. They behaved like slaves, taking every order as if it was the only thing they knew had to do.

He pulled out several pages from his drawer and read a specific page.

"I may have to try this," Hornsbury said to himself.

"They are becoming rebellious, I can't have that now can I?" he asked himself while looking in the mirror.

Chapter 20

"I wonder how much longer we have left," said Angela.

"Well, we only left three hours ago," Soriya replied.

"How do you know that?" asked Angela.

"Been singing songs in my head, I know how long each song is," replied Soriya, as she smiled at Jimmy.

"Do you sing also?" asked Jimmy.

"Yep, I'm also part of the church choir," answered Soriya.

"Angela's too scared to join," she teased.

"No, I'm not, I just don't think I can sing that well," replied Angela. Soriya laughed.

"Oh stop it."

"Well after we stop Hornsbury, maybe you can sing while I play the piano," Jimmy smiled at Soriya.

She of course smiled back.

"Of course," she then blushed.

Suddenly Jimmy felt sad. He knew that Soriya couldn't go back to his world.

He then took a deep breath and just decided to enjoy the time he could spend with her.

Chris started mumbling under his breath and clenched his fists.

"Okay, Jimmy I am starting to get scared," Soriya whispered to Jimmy. "Why?" asked Jimmy as he looked at Soriya.

Soriya's eyes moved to Chris.

"Chris, is everything okay?" asked Jimmy.

"I'm going to kill Hornsbury, come on we need to hurry!" shouted Chris.

"We must focus, no time for talking. Move!"

"Okay, you're not going to talk to us like that!" yelled Soriya.

"What has got into you?"

"You have become very angry since we left home," said Soriya.

"I am not repeating myself; you know why I am angry."

"And if you don't like it, you three can go on by yourselves," said Chris. "Hey what's your problem Chris?"

"Soriya's right, you have changed," said Jimmy.

"What exactly happened when you met that witch?" asked Soriya.
  "Come on Phillip, they're slowing us down," said Chris as he quickly moved ahead.
Phillip looked back at Angela, with a worried look on his face.

"Jimmy, we have to do something," said Soriya.

"Let's just get back, my uncle will know what to do," said Jimmy.
 Chris started to run and Phillip followed.
"He can't leave us!" shouted Angela, as she started to run.
"He has the spell!"
"No Angela!" shouted Jimmy, as he tried to pull Angela back.

"We'll be okay," said Jimmy.

"He's acting very strange and I don't want you two to be harmed."
 "Let's just keep the pace that we're at."
"We don't know where we are going, remember Phillip was leading us," replied Soriya.
"Don't worry, I've been marking the roads," assured Jimmy.

"You're so smart!" yelled Soriya as she hugged Jimmy and kissed him. "Come on you two lovebirds, you can kiss after we stop Hornsbury," said Angela.

"You don't think Chris is really going to kill him Jimmy do you?" asked Angela.
"I don't know, he has changed," said Jimmy.

"I know that what Hornsbury is doing is wrong but I don't think we should kill him."

"Now that Chris has the reversal spell, it just makes things more complicated." "I'm sure my uncle will know what to do though." "Come on, he is right about one thing, we must focus," said Jimmy. "We'll stay by your side Jimmy," said Angela.

"If Soriya trusts you, I trust you."

Sudddenly, for some strange reason, Soriya got a weird feeling in her gut, but dismissed it to nervousness.

"So what do you know about Olivia?" asked Soriya changing the subject.

"Well, I know my uncle may be falling in love with her," responded Jimmy. "Has your uncle ever been married?" asked Soriya.

"Yes, Once."

"Both his wife and son died." "His son would've been my age."

"I bet he's very happy that you're with him now," smiled Soriya.

"Yes, I think so too," said Jimmy.

"She seems really sweet, I think he should marry again," said Jimmy.

"Wait, you're the ones from the town, you should know more than I would," he added.

"I think she moved in with her sister," said Angela.

"Overheard my parents talking one day, she was trying to get work in their shop," she added.

"I wonder where she moved from," said Soriya.

"We'll find out when we get back I guess," replied Jimmy.
"How much longer do you think we have left?" asked Angela.
"I'm getting hungry," she added.
"Well, I think we're approaching another town," said Jimmy.
 "We can stop at a meat shop,"
"I'm getting hungry myself."

"You two are pigs, I'm still stuffed!" shouted Angela.

Angela was the thinnest of the group, and hardly ate a thing.

"You know, I really did see Phillip's father standing at the top of the stairs," Soriya said softly to Jimmy.
"I think we're all just very tired and scared," Jimmy responded.

"You heard Phillip's mom, his father is working," he added.

"I know what I saw, but maybe you're right," replied Soriya.
 "Besides, how can he be in two places at once?" asked Jimmy.
 "Unless he didn't really go to work," mumbled Soriya.
 "Okay, why wouldn't he have went to work?" asked Jimmy.
 "He seems like a responsible man."
"You sound so educated, where are you and your uncle from again?" asked Soriya.
Jimmy may have been close to poor but his mother taught him well.

He possessed intelligence as well.

However, Jimmy didn't know how to answer Soriya's question, as they weren't from her world.
"We're from far away," said Jimmy.
 "Oh look,"
"There's a town."

Soriya looked up at him with a confused look in her eyes.

She stopped herself from asking the question that deeply mattered to her, as she thought she knew what he would say. However, she didn't know whether or not it would be the truth.

The town the teens were approaching, was very small and only consisted of a few shops. There was a bakery, butcher shop, and what appeared to be a clothing store.
"This town looks deserted," said Soriya.
 "There's like no one out here."
"I feel sorry for the kids in this town, where's the candy?" asked Angela. "Candy rots your teeth silly," replied Soriya.
"Hey, candy every now and then isn't bad," laughed Angela.
 "So, where to Jimmy?" asked Soriya.
"Well, I don't know about you guys, but my stomach wants some meat," said Jimmy with an excited look.

Angela and Soriya turned and looked at each other,
"Men."
"I'm not a man yet," laughed Jimmy.

"Which is even worse!" shouted Soriya as she playfully shoved Jimmy.

"I hope they're open, I'm starving!" shouted Jimmy.

The girls followed Jimmy towards the butcher shop.

"Darnit, it doesn't open until 11 am," complained Jimmy.

"Well, what time is it?" asked Angela.

"Excuse me ma'am, would you by chance know what time it is?" Jimmy asked as an older woman passed by.

"It must not be that deserted," he said as he looked at Soriya.

"Well, there's the clock right in the town center," the older lady answered as she pointed.

"So, I'm assuming you three want some meat."

"Shop opens in ten minutes."

"Don't eat too much now," laughed the lady.

The older woman was very beautiful. She looked like she was in her forties, and was very slender with long black hair. Her skin tone was darker and stood medium height.

"You're not from around here I take it," said the woman.

"Why do you talk like that?" asked Angela.

"Angela!" yelled Soriya as she nudged Angela.

"It's okay," the woman said as she laughed.

"You sound different too," she said.

"My name is Miss Leslie."

"I'm Angela," said Angela. "Soriya," said Soriya. "Jimmy," said Jimmy.

"May I ask a question Miss Leslie?" asked Jimmy.

"As long as it's not about my age,"
"Sure!" smiled Miss Leslie.

"How far are we away from Harmony Town?" asked Jimmy.
 "Harmony what?" Miss Leslie replied.
"Harmony Town, it should be the next town," Soriya chimed in.

"Oh I'm sorry darlings, I've never been outside of this town,"
replied Miss Leslie. "She should still know where the next town is
located," mumbled Angela.
 "Mommy,mommy! Look what we found!" shouted two small
children running up to the woman.
The little girl was holding out a coin of some kind.
"Children, don't you see me talking?" she asked her children.
 "Sorry," said the little boy.
Both children looked like Miss Leslie. The girl had short brown
hair with a lighter complexion. The boy had a medium complexion
with a short haircut. However, both highly resembled their mother.
"Tell these lovely visitors your names," said Miss Leslie.
 "I'm James," said the boy.
"I'm Stacy," said the girl.

"Well nice to meet you," grinned Soriya as she extended her
hand.
 "Would you like some food?" she asked.
"No no, they just ate," replied Miss Leslie.

"We just ate hash browns, eggs, pancakes, and bacon!" said
Stacy.

"That sounds delicious!" said Jimmy, almost drooling from his mouth.

"We just ate too silly," laughed Soriya.

"About four hours ago," said Jimmy.

"Well, we really have to get going," said Miss Leslie.

"It was nice meeting you all!" she exclaimed.

"Thanks, you too!" shouted the three.

"Well she was nice," smiled Soriya.

"We should've asked her for a place to stay," Angela mumbled.

"I'm getting tired."

"Wait!" suddenly, Soriya ran after Miss Leslie.

"Excuse me ma'am," said Soriya, as she caught up. Miss Leslie looked at her.

"Yes, dear?"

"I don't mean to scare you, but if a strange man comes to your town, planning to have a concert..."

"Please tell everyone not to go."

"Well, why would I do that?" asked Miss Leslie.

"He's evil."

"He's going around trying to possess towns." "He's trying to take over our world as we know it.

"Oh my," said Miss Leslie as she put her hand on her mouth. She looked at her children and stated,

"Well thank you for warning me." "I will certainly look out for him."
"Do you know why he's doing it?"
"He wants power," Soriya replied.

"But I have to go now." "Please don't forget us."
"I surely won't," said Miss Leslie. "And good luck."
"Thank you," replied Soriya.
Soriya ran back toward the others.
"What was that all about?" asked Angela. "Warning her, you know," Soriya responded. "Just in case."
"Yep, that is a very good idea," Angela mumbled.

Soriya couldn't tell if Angela was being sarcastic or genuine.
"I think it was a good idea," smiled Jimmy.

Soriya smiled back at him, happy that he had approved.
"I'm so tired," moaned Angela.
"Well, let's eat and then see if we still want to rest afterwards," said Jimmy. "Sounds like a plan to me," said Angela.
Suddenly, the sign on the door was flipped around.
"Yes! They're open," said Jimmy.
"Calm down hungry boy," said Soriya.

Jimmy opened the door for the girls to enter first with Soriya smiling at the gesture.

"Good Morning Y'all!" shouted the man at the counter. The man stood about six feet tall with a medium build. He had a very friendly face and was excited to help.

"What can I get for ya?" he asked.
"Sausages and hot dogs!" shouted Jimmy.
"Okay son," laughed the butcher.
"How many pounds of the sausage would you like?"
"Well, we only have a little bit of money," answered Jimmy.
"We're from the next town," he added.
"Oh, so you've been doing some traveling."
"Don't worry, it's on me," smiled the butcher.
"Name's Tommy."
"I'll make sure you all have enough to eat," he added.

"Thanks sir!" exclaimed Jimmy.
"Don't worry."
"I have three kids about your ages."

"They have appetites just like yours," he laughed.
"Well, here you go."
"Have a safe journey," he said as he handed them the meat.

The three then started their journey back home. Well, for Jimmy, back to where he and the Music Man magically appeared.

Chapter 21

"How much longer do you think we have?" asked Angela.

"Not much further I suppose," replied Jimmy.
"Based on my memory, I think maybe a couple of hours."
"Are you scared?" asked Angela as she looked at Jimmy.
"Scared of what?" asked Jimmy.

"What Hornsbury might be capable of," replied Angela.

"How do we know he doesn't have more spells?" she also asked.
"You're right, we don't but we have to try to stop him," said Jimmy.
"Otherwise your family and friends won't be themselves any
longer," he added. "To be honest, I'm more scared of Chris than
anything," said Soriya.
"He has changed," she added.

"Well I haven't known him for that long," said Jimmy.
"But I think he just wants to harm Hornsbury," he added.
"Yeah, I guess you're right," replied Soriya.
"Besides, I'll protect you," said Jimmy as he smiled at Soriya.
"You too Angela," he added.

Angela looked up and smiled.

"You're so lucky Soriya," whispered Angela.

"I wonder what Hornsbury is doing now," Soriya said out loud.
"Who knows," replied Angela.
"But I'm sure it's not good," she added as she shook her head.

Indeed, Hornsbury was looking over a few pages of spells in his dressing room. "I don't understand why they are becoming rebellious," he said to himself, referring to the possessed teens. "I said the spell correctly.".

"I need to pay that witch another visit," he added.
"There's not enough time!"
He sighed.
"Hmm, I'll just have to re-cast this spell."

The original spell Hornsbury casted on his orchestra was a lengthy one. "Now, how am I going to gather them in a room all at once?" he asked himself out loud.

"During our final rehearsal!" he shouted.

"That way they can't mess up the performance," he added. "I've worked too hard and long for this."
"The world will soon be mine!" he shouted as he took a bow.

    Chris and Phillip seemed to know their way back to town.
 "So how did it feel seeing your mom again?" asked Chris.
 "I don't know," replied Phillip.
"It felt weird, maybe it's because I'm a ghost," Phillip added, with a sad look on his face.
"Well if she actually loves you then that shouldn't matter honestly Phillip," replied Chris.

"I don't like your dad all that much, he didn't seem too happy to be around you."
"Why do you say that?" asked Phillip.

"He barely spoke, you didn't notice?" asked Chris.
"No, I didn't," answered Phillip.
"I say you just stay with my family," Chris suggested.

"It's just my dad and I, mom died a long time ago.".

"You don't think your dad wouldn't mind if a ghost was living in his house?" asked Phillip.
"Trust me, he wouldn't," said Chris with a sly look on his face.
"We could always hide you!" he shouted.

"Does he know about Hornsbury?" asked Phillip.
"Of course he does, he doesn't like him," said Chris.
"Will he help us?" asked Phillip.
"We don't need any help," replied Chris.

"You must not know what he's capable of," said Phillip.
"He visited that witch quite often.".
"Well I visited her too, trust me, he won't hurt another soul," said Chris. "Have faith in me Phillip," he added.
"The others were annoying, well the girls were."

"Jimmy's okay, but he's stuck to Soriya's hip practically," said Chris.

"And that Soriya asks too many questions," he added.

"What's wrong with that?" asked Phillip.

"She's never been in this situation before," he added.

"I'll tell you what's wrong with that," replied Chris.

"She should've just let us boys do the talking," he added.

"I don't see why that matters, she seems pretty smart," rebutted Phillip.

"Do you want to go back there with them!!?" shouted Chris in an enraged manner. "They're probably lost," he joked.

"I was just saying, she probably knows more than we think is all," said Phillip.

"Well I don't like her," replied Chris.

"Was the witch scary?" Phillip asked, changing the subject.

"Not really, just frustrating," Chris replied.

"Well she is into witchcraft, which means she's probably evil," Phillip responded.

"She probably wants Hornsbury to follow through with his plan."

"Well he won't, not now," said Chris.

"And we don't have to worry about that witch anymore either."

"What do you mean?" Phillip asked.

"Let's just say, her services are permanently down," snickered Chris.

Phillip looked at Chris with a disturbed look on his face.

No one messed with the town witch. She was well over a century old, and her mother before her lived to be around 200. Her mother was burned at the stake for practicing witch craft and her daughters witnessed it.

What most townspeople didn't know was that there was a protection spell that their mother casted against the town. No one could harm them. Sadly though, the witch's sister, Anelia, died accidentally. She simply tripped and hit her head against an exposed pipe in their house.

The other witch, Priala, just kept to herself, making her potions and spells.

Chapter 22

"Let's rest and eat," said Jimmy, as he looked around for an area for them to rest at.

"Sounds good to me," said Soriya.

"I don't know about you two, but I don't see any benches or chairs," said Angela.

"Are you serious?" asked Soriya.

"I have a blanket in my bag," she added. "We will simply have a picnic."

"I suppose," replied Angela.

Soriya pulled the blanket out of her bag and pointed at a nearby lake. "We can have a picnic there," she said with a smile.

Angela followed Jimmy and Soriya to the location. "I have a bad feeling about this," said Angela.

"We're going to have a picnic, what could possibly go wrong?" Soriya asked. Soriya spread out the blanket on the grass, and instructed Jimmy to get out the food.

Jimmy's mouth watered as he stared at the selection of meats the butcher packed for them.

"What was that?" whispered Angela.

"What was what?" asked Soriya who was very focused on helping Jimmy lay out the meats.

"I heard a whisper," said Angela.

"Well we're the only three here silly," replied Soriya.

"What did you say you saw when we left Phillip's house?" asked Angela. "His dad, I don't think he really went to work," said Soriya. "How does he get to work?" asked Angela.

"Phillip's mom said he rides a bicycle," answered Jimmy.

"There it is again, you guys didn't just hear that?" asked Angela.

"I did," whispered Soriya.

"What do you think it is?" Angela asked.

"Well we have, or should I say had a ghost in our party," said Soriya.

"It could be anything.".

"Well while you two are trying to figure out where the imaginary sounds are coming from, I'm going to eat your sausages," said Jimmy as he was stuffing his mouth.

"I'm going to find out what it is," said Angela as she stood up.

"I'm going with you," replied Soriya, also standing up.

"Jimmy!" shouted Soriya.

"Guys, I'm sure it's nothing," said Jimmy, who would rather eat.

Soriya placed her hands on her hips, waiting for Jimmy to accompany them. "I thought you said you'd protect me?" Jimmy sighed.

"Where do you think it's coming from?" he asked.
"The forest?" asked Angela in a very low voice.
"Oh no, we are not going in there," said Jimmy.
"We have to get back to town."
"The concert is tomorrow," he added.

"They'll be much worse things than whispers if we don't get to Hornsbury in time."
The girls agreed and followed Jimmy back to eat their meals.

As soon as Angela was going to eat a piece of sausage, she heard the whisper again and looked straight up.
"The bird, it's a bird!" shouted Angela.
"Birds whisper?" asked Soriya.
"I've never heard a bird whisper before."

"Quick, Soriya, give me a piece of bread," said Angela as she stared at the bird. "We really don't have time for this," answered Soriya as she reached in the bag for a piece of bread.
Just as Soriya tried to start feeding the bird, a flock of birds swooped down and formed a line.
The three teenagers looked in shock, confused.

The birds formed a straight line, with the bird that Angela first met, being the leader.

The birds started to walk towards the nearby forest. What happened next made Angela shriek, the last bird turned around and whispered "follow".

"Oh no, we are NOT going in there," said Jimmy. "Come on, let's go," said Angela.

Angela was mesmerized at the little creatures and decided to follow them. "Angela, we really don't have time for this," said Soriya.

Angela ignored Soriya and started to follow the birds. Soriya, being the friend that the she was, decided to follow Angela, ignoring Jimmy's impatience. "Come on Jimmy, it'll be an adventure!" exclaimed Soriya.

Jimmy shook his head and followed.

"Ok, if I sense any danger, we have to go."

The forest was creepy indeed.

The birds stopped in front of two high trees. Both trees were more than ten feet tall with trunks were more than ten inches wide.

"Who have you brought here?" said one of the trees.

"Oh my!" gasped Soriya.

"This is not real,"

"This is not happening."

Angela even now had a confused look on her face. "We're just on our way home," said Angela.

"From where?" asked the tree.

"The last person who was here, was a witch, who casted a spell on some of our friends," the tree added.

"She pretended that she was here to help us, but she casted a spell instead."

Soriya suddenly looked at Jimmy.

She knew that it was the same witch that Christopher visited, or at least she hoped.

"What happened to your friends?" asked Soriya.

"They're dead," said the other tree, as a tear began to fall from its eyes. This tree seemed older, as the mouth drooped and the eyes looked very sad.

The other tree began to speak,

"Our animal friends are becoming instinct." "Not many of them left."

"And she killed some of them and took them." Angela gulped.

"Again, what brings you here?" asked the tree.

"We were just following your bird friends," said Angela. The birds began to whisper to the trees.

"Ah, the whispering birds think that you all may be in danger and may need help."

"How could they know?" Soriya began to ask.

"Why, our friends just know," said the younger tree as a smile formed. "Now, what are you all in danger of?"

"We," began Soriya.

"We are leaving now, it was nice meeting you all, but we really have to go," interrupted Jimmy as he reached for Soriya's hand.

"Jimmy they're trying to help us!" screamed Soriya.

"This witch that you speak of," Soriya continued to speak.

"She also gave a spell to a very cruel man who wants to possess people through music and we are trying to stop him."
"I wish there was something we could do," said the younger tree.
"Let's just go guys," said Jimmy.
"There's nothing they can do for us."
Soriya sighed in disappointment.
"I'm sorry about your animal friends," she said.

"I hope whatever the witch did, that you all stop her," replied the older tree. The three teenagers then went on their way, not wasting any more time.

Chapter 23

"Father!" shouted Chris from the bottom of the stairs, after he swung open the front door.
The door was never locked. There wasn't much crime in their town, except for children stealing candy every now and then.
"I wish he were here, don't want to scare him when he does arrive," said Chris. Phillip looked around the house and noticed how tidy it was.
"Your house is really clean."

"Reminds me of my house," continued Phillip.
"Are you hungry?" asked Chris.
"Looks like father made a pot of stew," said Chris as he licked his lips. For some reason, Phillip felt uneasy being in Chris's house, but he couldn't understand why.
"Are we going to see the others?" asked Phillip. "Others?" asked Chris.

"Jimmy and the girls," said Phillip. "What for?" asked Chris. "All they do is slow us down."

"If I'm not mistaken, the concert is tomorrow." "So we need to prepare!"

"Well shouldn't we meet up with the others and make a plan?" asked Phillip. "Don't worry, I have the spell," Chris replied. "We can stop him," he added.

"I still think we should see the others," said Phillip. "You're a ghost, you can go try to find them," Chris snapped back. "But I don't think you will, they may be lost," he added with a smile.

At this point, Phillip no longer wanted to be around Chris. The fact that he was okay with the others being lost, if they were indeed lost, disturbed Phillip.

"Anyway, I'm tired," said Chris, as he plopped on the sofa.

"Ghosts eat right?" he asked as he was falling asleep. "Get some stew and rest, we have a big day ahead of us tomorrow." Before Phillip knew it, Chris was sound asleep, snoring loudly.

Phillip didn't know what to do; he hadn't planned for everyone to separate. "I sure hope they make it back safely," he whispered to himself.

He then decided to just go look for them. Chris was sound asleep and Phillip didn't expect him to awake anytime soon. Just as Phillip was getting ready to leave, he stopped and looked at Chris. He wanted to see the spell for himself. Phillip shook his head at the idea and decided not to look at it in fear of what power it might possess. Phillip looked back at Chris before he opened the door. "I sure hope he comes to his senses," he said out loud. "We need all of the help we can get," he added.

Unsure of what to expect, Phillip took a deep breath and opened the front door. Chris suddenly woke up at the noise and ran to the door to confirm his suspicion of what just took place. Chris had confirmed that Phillip indeed left, and he became very upset. "I'm the one with the spell, they're all fools," Chris said to himself. "Fools!" he shouted, as he slammed the door.

Chapter 24
"Look!"
"We're almost there!" shouted Angela. Soriya and Jimmy were holding hands as they all started to pick up the pace. "The concert is tomorrow right?" asked Soriya. "Yes," said Jimmy. "Do you think Phillip and Chris are already there?" Soriya also asked. "If they are, I'm sure Chris has another agenda," said Angela. "Well we just need to get to my uncle, he'll know what to do," said Jimmy. "I sure hope so," replied Soriya.

"I don't know who I'm more afraid of; Chris or Hornsbury," she added. Jimmy looked at Soriya and for some reason, agreed with her.

Phillip didn't know what to do, or where to go. Sure, he should find the others to make them aware of the rehearsal. "I have to go find them, they have to be near," Phillip said to himself.
Phillip didn't know at the time, but he was correct. The others were now at the house of the Music Man.
"I don't think he's in there Jimmy," said Angela.

"We've been knocking for five minutes," added Soriya. "Where else would we go?" asked Jimmy.
Suddenly, the door opened, and the Music Man smiled.

"You all made it back!" he shouted as he kissed Soriya and Angela both on the cheek.
"Never leave like that again!" the Music Man shouted, as he looked at the teens.
"I was so afraid for you all!"
"I'm sorry uncle," Jimmy said softly.
"We didn't think you would let us go."
There was an awkward silence.
Suddenly, Olivia walked out with a cake in her hands.
"It's time to celebrate!" she shouted.

"What's the occasion?" asked Angela with an annoyed expression on her face. "Is it one of your birthdays'?" she added.
"Jimmy, you should've told us!" she smiled. "No no," said Olivia.
"But it IS a special occasion," she smiled.

The room fell silent. "Uncle tell us," said Jimmy, in an impatient manner.
"We're getting married!" shouted Olivia.

Angela looked at Soriya, and Soriya looked at Jimmy. Jimmy did not say anything, he just looked confused. "Wow," said Angela, with a smirk on her face.
"That was quick," she added.

Angela was the blunt one of all of them, and she was annoyed at the fact that a wedding was the topic of the discussion.
"Jimmy, maybe we should ask him now," Angela said as she leaned towards Jimmy.
They were all sitting on the sofa, with Jimmy between Angela and Soriya.

"Yes, Uncle, we have some news," said Jimmy.

"But first, congratulations!"

"I know you really love her," he added, as he looked at Olivia.

The Music Man nodded in agreement and was very appreciative of Jimmy's acknowledgement of the odd situation.
"Thank you my boy."

"Now what's the news?" he asked Jimmy.
"Well, we have the spell," Jimmy replied.
"What he means is that CHRIS has the spell," interjected Soriya.
 "He has the reversal spell and we don't know where he has gone."
"He made Phillip go with him and he has changed very much."
"Hm," said the Music Man.

"So what are you all going to do?" he asked.

"Well that's what we're here to ask you," said Jimmy. "What should we do?" he asked.
"I think you should go find Chris, as he has the spell." "That's just it sir, we don't know where he's at," said Jimmy. "I bet he's at home," said Angela.

"Think about it," she added.

"Where else would he go?" she asked.

"Angela has a good point Jimmy," said the Music Man. "He's not going to just give it to us," said Jimmy.
"Which is why you should ask him to work together," said the Music Man. "You don't understand," replied Soriya.
"He has changed," she added.

"What other options do you all have?" asked the Music Man.
"Well, can you help us?" asked Jimmy in a quiet voice.
The Music Man looked up at Olivia.

Jimmy thought to himself about the conversation that had taken place between them, in private.
He remembered that the Music Man said he would get them back home. Jimmy loved Soriya but he also still missed his home very much, including his mother.
Jimmy was indeed disappointed with the Music Man for getting distracted.

He was very happy that the Music Man had fallen in love but there were much more important things to accomplish.

Soriya looked at Jimmy and saw the confusion on his face and began to speak.

However Jimmy stated very quickly, "People will become possessed sir."

"You don't know what type of power Hornsbury holds." "I doubt that he only knows that one spell," added Jimmy.

"What should we do?" asked the Music Man.

Jimmy wasn't sure as to how to answer the Music Man's question; he had never been in this situation before.

"We need the spell," interrupted Soriya.

"So can you come with us?" asked Jimmy, while looking at the Music Man. "Do I have a choice?" asked the Music Man.

"Like you said, people will get hurt," he added.

Jimmy nodded in agreement with the Music Man and quickly stood up.

"We don't have time to waste," said Jimmy.

"We'll go to Chris's house together," he added. "What about Phillip?" asked Soriya.

"What do you mean?"

"He's with Chris," said Jimmy. "No he's not," said Angela.

"He's at the door," she added as she pointed.

They all turned and looked at the door, and sure enough, Phillip was there.

Chapter 25

Jimmy walked to the door, as it was partially open, surprised to see Phillip by himself.
"Where's Chris?" asked Jimmy.
It was very windy outside for some strange reason.

"I left him back at the house, he's acting very strange," Phillip responded. "Oh my poor boy, surely you're cold," said Olivia.
"I didn't think ghosts get cold," joked Angela.

"Or do they?" she asked, second guessing herself.

"I'm fine, but Chris is the least of our worries," said Phillip.
"Hornsbury is already rehearsing."
"Oh no," said Soriya as she looked at Jimmy. "Well the concert is tomorrow," said Jimmy. "This is why we must go get Chris."
"He has the spell, and only the spell can stop him." "Or we could simply kill him," said Phillip.
"Now now, that's not the right thing to do," said the Music Man.
"Well pardon me sir but you're not the one who's dead," said Phillip.

"Well it doesn't make it right to go killing people," said the Music Man. "That's easy for you to say, you're still alive," said Phillip.

"Do you know what it's like to not be able to hug your mother, or your baby brother?" cried Phillip.

"No, but killing Hornsbury won't bring you back either," the Music Man responded.

"Enough!" shouted Soriya.

"I am tired of the arguing, we are wasting time!" she added. Jimmy looked at Soriya, surprised that she could get that upset.

"I just want this to be over with," Soriya said.

"You speak of your brother and mother Phillip, but I miss my family as well," she added.

"We are doing nothing by standing here arguing." "What time is it anyway?" she asked.

"About five," said the Music Man.

"You see, we've already been here for a hour," said Soriya.

"Where's Olivia?" asked the Music Man, realizing that she had disappeared. The Music Man got up and searched for her throughout the house.

"Where did she go?" he asked out loud.

"You see, strange things keep happening," said Angela. "We'll disappear next," she added.

"Maybe, Chris has brought bad luck to us all."

"Don't think like that," Soriya snapped. "Hmm let's see," Angela started to say.

"You saw Phillip's father when he was supposedly at work." "Chris has became someone else."

"And oh, Mr. Cornelius's lover has disappeared." "Yep, things are looking up."

"And the icing on the cake, we're trying to stop a powerful man from taking over the world," said Angela.

"Yep, this is absolutely wonderful!" she shouted.

"SHUT UP!" yelled Soriya.

"That's it, I am going to Chris's," Soriya stated as she looked at each of them.

"Anyone else want to join?" she asked.

Jimmy, confused at Soriya's temper, ran to her side hoping that she would calm down.

"It's going to be okay," said Jimmy, as he stared into her eyes.

"Is it?" she asked him back.

"Yes, I won't let him hurt your family," said Jimmy.

"Why would they go to his concert anyway?" asked Angela. "That wouldn't be a good idea," she added.

"My father signed an agreement with Hornsbury, he's one of the ushers," Soriya said quietly.

"What!" exclaimed Angela.

"Why haven't you told us?" she asked. "I didn't want to scare you all," replied Soriya.

"I didn't want you thinking that my father was helping him."

"This happened before we found out what Hornsbury was up to," said Soriya. "I am scared," she added as tears fell from her eyes. "Mother will be there as well." "I'm so scared."
"My father has signed an agreement, and he won't believe us if I try to warn him." Soriya started to cry hysterically, while Jimmy looked to the Music Man for answers.

"Don't worry dear," said the Music Man, in a reassuring manner. "Nothing will happen to your family."
"Let's go," he stated as he began to walk towards the door.

"What about Olivia?" asked Jimmy.

"She has vanished without a trace," he added.

"I think she went out the back door, she's scared as well," said the Music Man. "She probably went to make sure her sister is okay."
"Come along now."
"Hornsbury must be stopped."
And just like that, Soriya, Angela, Phillip, and Jimmy followed the Music Man's lead.
They all were walking to Chris's house, in a fast pace.

"I'm nervous," said Soriya to Jimmy.

"Don't worry, my uncle and I will protect you," said Jimmy.
"Besides, we have the one thing that can stop him," he added.
"Not yet," said Angela.
"What if Chris says no?" she also asked.

"She may be right Jimmy, he's been acting very strange," said Phillip.

"Hey hey, we'll just find out when we get there," said the Music Man.

Hornsbury had everything ready for the concert. It was a free concert and he just wanted everyone to come. He set up the music stands and decorated the stage as well.

"The rehearsal will start in one hour," he said to himself.

"The ushers will be here very soon." "They better not mess this up for me."

Hornsbury then took another bow and exited his dressing room.

The Music Man and the teenagers were on their way to Chris's house when suddenly Jimmy accidentally bumped into a little girl, a Harmonian of course.

"Excuse me little one," Jimmy said.

"I'm sorry."

"Are you excited for Hornsbury's concert?" asked the little girl.

"She can't stop talking about him," laughed her mother.

Jimmy just stared at the little girl deciding whether or not to warn them.

"Jimmy, we have to go!" shouted Soriya.

"Wait."

"Don't go to his concert," said Jimmy.

"But why wouldn't we?" asked the girl's mother. "Hornsbury is evil," Jimmy replied.

"Please don't go."

The little girl's mother grabbed her daughter's hand.
"Come on let's go sweety."
The little girl looked back at Jimmy with a scared look on her face.
"Come on Jimmy!" shouted Soriya, as she grabbed his hand. "We have to go!"
Jimmy looked at the little girl one more time and then followed Soriya.

The group finally made it to Chris's house and the Music Man wasted no time knocking on his door.
"Who is it?" a voice asked behind the door.
Surprised that there was an answer so suddenly,

"It's Mr. Cornelius, I'd like to talk to you," said the Music Man.
"About what?" replied Chris.
"It's cold out here son, would you be so kind to let me in?" asked the Music Man. "I'd like some warm tea," he added.

"Well we don't have any."

"And I'm not your son," said Chris. "Chris," said the Music Man.
"Look Jimmy," said Soriya, as she pointed.
Suddenly, Chris's father started to walk up.
"Well hello there Cornelius,"
"You've got theeee?… "

"Wait, are you a gh-gh?" asked Chris's father, as he stared at Phillip. "Yes, I'm a ghost," answered Phillip.

"How may I help you all?" asked Chris's father, still disturbed at the fact there was a ghost standing right in front of him. "Where's Chris?"

"He's in there sir," said Jimmy.

"It's cold, come come, we'll all have tea," Chris's father said, as he turned the key and opened the door.
They all entered the house.

"You can't come in here!" shouted Chris, as he walked toward the stairs. "Son, why are you yelling?" asked his father.
"They can't come in here, I have to leave," said Chris.
"Sir, we have come to see Chris," said the Music Man.

"He has something that we really need."

"It is very important and the citizens of this town can be in very real danger if we do not get it."
"Chris, what is he talking about?" asked Chris's father. Suddenly Soriya spoke,
"Sir, it's Mr. Hornsbury, he's trying to possess the world with his music." "And your son, has the spell to stop him from doing so," said Soriya. "She's lying, I have no such thing," said Chris.
"You're lying Chris," snapped Angela.

"We all went to the town where Mr. Hornsbury came from, to get the spell from the witch," said Angela.
"The witch?" asked Chris's father. "Spells are nothing to play with son."

170

"If this is true what you're friends are saying, then you must give it to them." "Mr. Cornelius is your conductor, you must respect him and help him." "No!" shouted Chris.

"I'm sorry about being angry with you earlier Cornelius," said Mr. McClain. "But if magic is involved, then by all means I will help you."

Suddenly, Chris started to run towards the couch. Jimmy put out his foot and Chris went flying through the air.

"I'm sorry sir, had no other choice," said Jimmy to Chris's father. Chris's father nodded.

The Music Man pulled out a rope from his pocket and hurried and tied Chris's hands.

Jimmy then proceeded to search Chris's pockets in hope of finding the spell. "It's not here," said Jimmy, disappointed.

"You'll never find it," snickered Chris.

"Chris, why are you doing this?" asked his father.

Chris, deciding not to answer, turned his head and became silent.

"Check the couch," said Phillip.

Without hesitation, Jimmy search the couch and indeed found the ripped page. "Got it!" he shouted.

"Come on, we have no time to waste!" he shouted as they all went running toward the school. "Well here we go!" shouted Angela to Soriya.

"What do you think is going to happen?" she also asked. "I don't know."

"I'm just hoping for the best," said Soriya.

"Come on, let's go this way," said Phillip, as he and Jimmy led the way. They picked up the pace, knowing they had no time to waste.
Suddenly, Angela slipped and fell.

"Ouch!"

"Oh goodness," she mumbled as she observed the large rock that made her fall. "Are you okay?" asked Jimmy, as he noticed that the others fell behind.
"Yes," said Angela, as she got up and dusted herself off. "Are you bruised?" asked Soriya.
"I don't think so," said Angela. "It just hurts," she added.
The teens then proceeded to enter the school, not knowing what to expect.

Chapter 26

"Come on," said Phillip. "This way."
"Hear that?" asked Jimmy.

"Sounds like music," said the Music Man. "They're rehearsing!" shouted Jimmy.
"So what's the plan boys?" asked the Music Man. "We need to destroy the potion and go into the
auditorium," Phillip answered.
"We can't all just go in the auditorium," Jimmy interjected.
"He could be expecting us." "I'll go first," said Phillip. "He'll be shocked to see me."

"I'll be a diversion," he added. "And as he's focused on me,"
"You chant the spell," he said as he looked at Jimmy. "You all
enter from the backstage."
"And I'll enter from the auditorium doors." "Understood?"
"Sounds good to me," said Jimmy.

"What about the potion?" interjected Soriya. "We'll go destroy that
now," said Phillip.
Phillip looked at the girls and then at the Music Man. They all
nodded in agreement.
"Okay, it's time," said Phillip.

The teens and the Music Man made their way to Hornsbury's
dressing room, in a hurried manner.
 "Okay, let's all search for the potion," Phillip said, as they entered
the room.
They began searching for the potion. "Wait."
"What was that noise?" whispered Soriya. "What noise?" asked
Jimmy.
"What are you guys doing?" asked an unfamiliar voice.

They all looked up, and one of the twins entered the room.

"What are you guys doing?" "You shouldn't be here." They all
looked at each other.
"Is that you Phillip?" John, the twin, asked. "What happened to
you?"
"Hornsbury put a spell on me," Phillip responded.

"We're trying to stop him."

"I can't let you do that," said John. "Move out of the way John," said Phillip. "He can't do this."

Suddenly, Jimmy tackled John. "Help you guys," shouted Jimmy. Soriya found a piece of rope and they tied him up. "He can't do this John," cried Phillip.

"He just can't." "You're under a spell." "You will see."

"You're not going to get away with this!" shouted John, as he squirmed around. "I found it!" shouted Angela, as she held the infamous potion in her hand.

"Okay, let's break it!" shouted Jimmy. Jimmy grabbed the potion and immediately destroyed it.

"Okay, let's go you all," said Phillip.

"We have no time to waste."

"I'm sorry John, but we have to stop him," Phillip said, as he looked back at John quickly.

"You'll see!" he shouted.

The teens and the Music Man proceeded to walk towards the auditorium, in a very nervous manner. In fact, Jimmy kept fidgeting, as he didn't know what to expect.

"Okay, let's split up," said Phillip.

"It's time."

Chapter 27

Phillip took deep breaths and entered the auditorium.
 Hornsbury was standing on the stage and looked right at him.

"How?"
"How?" asked Hornsbury several times.
"How can you be a...a..?"
"A what!?" shouted Phillip.

"A ghost?!"

"How did you get here?" asked Hornsbury.

"You killed me but my spirit lives on!" shouted Phillip.

Hornsbury's band started to chatter, looking at Hornsbury and then back at Phillip.
"Quiet!" shouted Hornsbury.
"You can't stop me boy!"

"Your plan stops here!" Jimmy suddenly shouted.

Hornsbury looked to the right of him and Jimmy began chanting the spell. The teenagers and the Music Man were all standing there, watching.
 "You worthless child!" shouted Hornsbury.
Suddenly, Hornsbury began chanting another spell, and pulled out a wand.

He looked right at the Music Man.

The Music Man then fell.

He tried to get back up but he was stuck.

"Look!" shouted Angela as she pointed to the doors.

Suddenly, the whispering birds from the forest flew through the auditorium and swarmed Hornsbury.
"Stop him!" cried Soriya. The birds whispered, "Stop…Stop…"
Hornsbury couldn't see and grabbed one of the birds and threw it to the ground.
"Get away from me!" he shouted.
"No!" shouted Soriya.

The bird hit the ground and broke his neck. Soriya ran to the bird, picked it up, and pet it. "I'm so sorry," she cried.
She kissed it and looked up at Hornsbury.
  "You're an evil, evil man!" she cried.
Hornsbury continued to chant while fighting the birds. "Hurry!" Soriya shouted to Jimmy.
"He can't get away with this!"

Suddenly, Olivia came running through the doors.
"No!!!!!!!!!!!" she shouted.
She ran up the stage, breathing heavily. The Music Man stared at her in awe.
She rushed over to him and looked up at Hornsbury. "You have to stop this!" she screamed.
Soriya looked at Angela.

"How did she ?"

"Where have you been?!" shouted Hornsbury.

"You were supposed to lead him here at the time I told you to, now look what you have done!"

"What is he talking about?" asked the Music Man. Angela looked at Olivia and shouted, "What?!" "You were working with him this entire time?!"

"How could you do this?" the Music Man asked. "I loved you."

"I love you too Cornelius," Olivia cried.

"I love him!" she shouted as she looked at Hornsbury.

"I'm sorry Cornelius, you were under my spell," Olivia explained.

"I used magic when I was singing to you so that you would be under my control."

"So that Hornsbury could follow through with his plan."

"But enough is enough!" she shouted as she looked back up at Hornsbury.

"You can't do this!"

"Oh but I can!" shouted Hornsbury, as he began chanting another spell. "You're a traitor!" he added.

"Don't listen to him Cornelius, I fell in love with you and I choose you!"

"You will die too!" shouted Hornsbury.

"All of you!"

"But you will be the first to go," he said as he looked at the Music Man.

Hornsbury continued chanting his spell and pointed his wand at the Music Man.

The Music Man started to rise up.

Hornsbury had full control over him. The Music Man began

walking toward the front of the stage and fell backward. The stage was about ten feet high.
"No!!!!!!!!!!!!" shouted Olivia as she ran down to the Music Man.
"Jimmy hurry!" shouted Soriya.
Jimmy finally ended his chant, remaining focused.

Hornsbury redirected his attention to Jimmy but he was too late.
He started to slowly fade away into pieces.
"You will neverrrrr stoppppp me!!!" Hornsbury screamed, trying to point his

wand at Jimmy.

He was unsuccessful and suddenly, he was no more.

Olivia hovered over the Music Man, crying hysterically.

"I love you," said Olivia.

"Please hang in there," she added.

"I…I love you too," said the Music Man, as he breathed heavily.
Jimmy and the others also ran over to him.
"Uncle!"

"No!"

"I'm sorry I couldn't help more Jimmy," said the Music Man. "No uncle, you did everything you could," said Jimmy. "Just fight, I've already lost my father, please hang on."

Suddenly, Hornsbury's band became themselves and rose up to help aid the Music Man.

The Music Man's breathing became much more frantic and then suddenly stopped.

His eyes were partly closed.

Angela checked the Music Man's pulse.

"He's gone," she said as she looked at Jimmy. "Mom taught me," said added.

Jimmy began crying hysterically. Soriya ran over to Jimmy to hug him.

"He's in a better place now," she cried as she hugged him very tightly. "It's okay."

Jimmy hugged her back.

Everyone else surrounded the Music Man, looking down at him.

"He was a very nice man," cried Phillip.

"I'm sorry about your uncle Jimmy," whispered Angela.

"He's not really my uncle," said Jimmy as he wiped the tears from his eyes. "What?" asked Olivia, in a shaky voice.

"We're from another world," said Jimmy.

"We were playing the piano, at Cornelius's house and we began to spin. And then, we arrived here."

"But I'm going to stay here and make music, as he did," he added.

Olivia looked down at the Music Man and then back up at Jimmy and ran. Angela ran after her to console her.

"I need to visit my mother though, to tell her I'm okay," Jimmy continued to say.

"I'll come with you," said Soriya.

"Okay," Jimmy responded.

"I sure wish there was a spell to make me alive again," Phillip interrupted. "But at least Hornsbury was stopped, I couldn't imagine what he would've done." "I think I want to go back to my family."

"I'm so glad I met you all."

"I'll never forget you."

"I'm sorry for your loss Jimmy."

Jimmy nodded his head.

"Thanks for all of your help Phillip," Jimmy said in a low voice.

Soriya hugged Phillip, as she cried. And Phillip walked away.

"Come on, let's go," Jimmy said, as he asked for Soriya's hand.

Both teens walked back up the stage, and paused.

They looked at the small remnants of Hornsbury.

"Thank you for saving us," said Soriya, as she kissed Jimmy.

"Phillip's right, who knows what could've happened."

"It wouldn't have been without Cornelius," said Jimmy. "He gave me courage, and let me come into his home." "I ran away from my mom."
"I felt as if she didn't love me anymore."

"But now I realize, she's just overwhelmed with all of her responsibilities."
"I want her to live here."
"We can stay in Cornelius's house."

The teens then made their way to the other school and found the piano. There it was, still in its original spot.
"All we have to do is play a song," said Jimmy.

    "Do you know how to play?" he asked.
"No, not really," answered Soriya. "I'll just play, it's okay," said Jimmy.
They both sat down, in front of the piano.
Jimmy placed his fingers on the keys, and began to play, as he had the piece memorized.
"Nothing's happening," said Soriya, with a confused look on her face.
 "I don't understand," Jimmy said.
"Jimmy, wasn't Cornelius at the piano too?" asked Soriya. "Yes."
"Yes he was," replied Jimmy.

"So that means you can't go back right?" asked Soriya.
Jimmy sat there in silence, with a tear falling from his eye.
"I'm sorry Jimmy."
"I know how terribly you must miss your mom," said Soriya.

Soriya got up from the bench and placed her hand on Jimmy's shoulder, to give him space.

Jimmy then stood up and took a deep breath, and began to walk away from the piano.

"You couldn't imagine living here?" joked Soriya.

"Of course I can," Jimmy said, as he tried to smile. "Well then, let's go," said Soriya.

Soriya grabbed Jimmy's hand, and he appreciated the fact that she cared so much for him.

They then made their way back to the other school. Jimmy quickly walked to where the Music Man laid.

"What are we going to do for Mr. Cornelius?" Jimmy asked.

"He deserves to have the best burial, he truly was a very honorable man," said Soriya.

"A hero," added Jimmy.

"I'll never forget you sir," said Jimmy, as a tear fell from his eye.

Angela walked back to the others, and stood next to Soriya.

"Is Olivia okay?" asked Soriya.

"No, she wouldn't talk to me," said Angela.

"I'm sorry you guys," said John, the twin, as he walked up.

"Thank you for stopping him."

"It's okay," said Soriya.

The band leader, Jennifer, also walked up.

She was very pretty with dark brown eyes, and olive skin. "What happened to me?"

"Where am I?"

"Why are we all here?!"

"You were all possessed," replied Angela. "But Hornsbury is no more."
"We didn't harm anyone did we?" asked Jennifer.

"No you did not," answered Angela.

"Can you show us how to get back home?" Jennifer asked.

"Of course we can," said Soriya with a warm smile. "I feel so bad for Phillip," said Jimmy.
"Don't," Angela quickly whispered and pointed.

They all looked up and sure enough, Phillip was right there. "I couldn't leave you guys," Phillip said in a low voice.
"You're not going back home?" asked Soriya.

"I don't know, I'd rather let them be at peace," said Phillip.
"Oh Phillip!" shouted Jennifer.
"What did Hornsbury do to you?"

"He murdered him Jennifer," said John.

"Hornsbury will not hurt another soul!" shouted Angela strongly.

Jimmy looked up and started to talk when Soriya suddenly pointed at a dark figure.

"Jimmy!!!!!!!!!!!!!" she screamed.

"I have found you and you're going to give it back to me!"

All four teenagers looked up, and Angela screamed in horror.

"I killed your father and will kill your mother and brother if you don't GIVE IT BACK!" the witch shouted, pointing at Phillip, backing him up into a corner.

"My mother and brother have done nothing wrong, deal with me instead!" shouted Phillip.

"Wait, give what back?" asked Jimmy nervously.

"My book!" the witch shouted.

"Your friend took my book and I want it back!"

"CHRIS!" whispered Soriya, as Angela looked at her.

"She must have been what I saw, moving behind Phillip's father, at the top of the stairs," said Soriya.

Angela gulped.

"But we don't know where he is," said Angela in a shaky voice.

"You're lying!" shouted the witch.

"Give my book back to me or I'll kill his mother and brother and cast a spell on all of you!" shouted the witch.

"Okay okay, Chris has it," Jimmy stated nervously.

"But honestly, we don't know where he put it." "Well take me to him and I'll deal with him!"

"But if he doesn't give it back, all of you will be no more!" shouted the witch. "Take me, NOW!"

Soriya quickly grabbed Jimmy's hand, frightened and confused.
Jimmy lead the witch and the others to Chris's home.
"His dad will let us in," said Jimmy as he knocked on the door.

There was no answer.

"That's strange," said Jimmy as he pressed his ear against the
door.

"I don't have time for this," the witch said, as she pointed her
wand at Jimmy. "Wait wait!" shouted Soriya, as she jumped in
front of Jimmy.
Jimmy was taken aback that Soriya would risk her life for him, he
stared at her, and spoke up against the witch.
"I have to kick down the door."
"Is that a problem for you?"
 "Hurry up, I just want my book."
"Stand back!" shouted Jimmy.
Suddenly, he stepped back and with all his might, kicked down
the door. "Ahhhhhhhhh!!!!!!!!" screamed Angela.
Chris's father was laying on the floor with his hands tied together.
 "You have to stop him!" shouted Mr. Mcclain.
"What did he do!?" cried Angela. "
Shh" whispered Jimmy.
"He's upstairs," he pointed.

They all walked up the stairs in a quiet manner, making sure not
to be heard. Soriya quickly covered her mouth and pointed.

Chris was holding the book in front of him, chanting a spell in the mirror.

"Give me my book!" shouted the witch.

"Or I'll kill your friends!"

Chris suddenly stopped chanting.

"NO."

"The book was in my knapsack all along."
"After I put it back into the grave, I thought to myself what kind of power it held."
"So I went back and took it."

"My father tried to stop me and look what happened to him."
"IT'S MINE," said Chris, in a determined and expressionless manner.
"They're not my friends."
"The book is now MINE."

"Chris! Give her the book!" shouted Angela.

Suddenly, the witch pulled out her wand and pointed it at Soriya.
"Nooooo!!!!!!" shouted Jimmy.

Chapter 28

Jimmy awoke, breathing heavily.

He looked around with sweat dripping from his forehead.

"What's wrong my boy?"

"Everything alright?"

Jimmy stared at the Music Man.

"You're. ..you're alive!" he shouted, as he jumped off the couch.

"Well I certainly hope so," said the Music Man.

"How did .." Jimmy said under his breath. He had the most confused look on his face.

"How did what my boy?" the Music Man asked.

"It was all a dream," Jimmy said to himself.

"What was a dream?" asked the Music Man. Jimmy just sat there, in silence.

He thought about Soriya, Angela, and Phillip.

"I'll miss them," he said quietly to himself, still in shock.

"Especially Soriya."

"Who's Soriya?" asked the Music Man. "It's nothing," said Jimmy.

"Can we make music?" asked Jimmy excitedly. "Become world famous conductors?!?"

"We both can play by ear!"

"We would be great!" shouted Jimmy.

"What's got into you my boy?" asked the Music Man.

He was taken aback by Jimmy's excitement and didn't understand where it all came from.

"Let's just make music," said Jimmy.

"Well why not?" asked the Music Man as he laughed. "We'll start tomorrow," he added.
Jimmy ran to the Music Man and hugged him. The Music Man embraced Jimmy, and laughed.
"Now you go back to bed, we have a bright and fun day ahead of us," said the Music Man.
Jimmy jumped back onto the couch, and tried to go back to sleep.

The Music Man just stared at the wall, and cherished his moment of happiness. Suddenly, there was a sudden knock on the door.
"I wonder who that could be," said the Music Man.
"I bet it's Ms. Lois," said Jimmy.
"I could sure eat her delicious cake right about now," said the Music Man. "Huh?" Jimmy asked.
Jimmy was so excited that he tuned the Music Man out.

It surprised Jimmy at how calm the Music Man always was. Even in Jimmy's dream, he was calm.
The Music Man opened the door and the voice coming from the other end startled Jimmy.
Jimmy walked towards the door, as the Music Man opened it more, and sure enough, it was his mother.
"My son!"

"I missed you so much."

Jimmy's mother embraced him tightly and cried hysterically.
"What were you thinking?!"

"Why did you run away?!"

"How did you find?" Jimmy started to ask.

Suddenly a cop spoke.
"We've been searching every house ever since you left son."
"Your mom thought something very bad happened to you."
"Cornelius Waters you are under arrest for holding this boy prisoner." "What!? NO!!!!!" Jimmy shouted.
"He let me in from the cold!"

"You don't know what you're talking about!"

"He has made you say those things Jimmy, it's okay, you're safe now," Jimmy's mother said as she took his hand.
"Mother no! I promise you. He has been very kind to me." Jimmy wished he had not awoke from his dream.
Not only did the Music Man die in Jimmy's dream but now he was about to be sent to jail in reality.
"You can't do this!" Jimmy shouted.

"Ask Ms. Lois, who lives next door!" "She'll tell you."
"Son, there's no one that lives next door," said the cop.
 "This is still a dream, this is still a dream."
Jimmy kept pinching himself.

"I'll go get my things," said the Music Man. "No!" shouted Jimmy as he ran after him.

"That won't be necessary," said the cop.

"We have clothes for you." "Mother, I'm telling you!" Jimmy cried.
"Go next door, you'll see for yourself." "We have just been playing the"

Jimmy looked back, and the piano wasn't there.

Suddenly, he closed his eyes and fell backwards, and his head hit the ground.

Jimmy woke up and looked around. He was breathing frantically.

"There's the piano!" he screamed.

"What?!"

"There were two dreams!"

"What's going on my boy?" asked the Music Man.

"Am I still dreaming?" Jimmy asked.

"Not that I know of," laughed the Music Man.

"I had two dreams sir."

"The first one, you died!"

"The second one, you were almost taken away by a cop." "My mom thought you wouldn't let me leave your home."

"I was so scared for you," cried Jimmy, with tears falling from his eyes.

"I think I'm going to go back home and let my mom know that I'm alright," said Jimmy.

"I think that's a very good idea," said the Music Man.

"And then when you come back, you can tell me all about your dreams," he added.

"Ok sir," said Jimmy as he gave the Music Man a hug.

"You're like a father to me now, and I'm glad I met you," said Jimmy. "I'm glad I met you too son," said the Music Man.
A tear fell from the Music Man's eye, as he was thankful that God had brought him another son, even if it wasn't his own.
Jimmy put on a pair of pants and a sweater, as it was a little chilly outside. "I'll be back sir," said Jimmy.
The door closed and the Music Man sat down at his piano, and started to play. Jimmy started to walk towards his home, not knowing what to expect when he appeared.

Chapter 29

"Hey there!" shouted Ms. Lois.

She was hanging clothes on a clothesline to dry. "Where are you off to?"
"Going to let my mother know that I'm okay," said Jimmy. "Yes, that's a very good idea."
"Here, let me give you some cake to take to her," said Ms. Lois. "It'll also make her happy."
"Does she like cake?" "Yes, yes she does," Jimmy replied.
"Well, come on in."
"Let me cut you a couple of slices," said Ms. Lois.

Jimmy and Ms. Lois went into her house and Jimmy noticed that Michael and Morris were not there.

"Where are your boys ma'am?" asked Jimmy. "Oh, they went into the city to buy some food." "Here you go."

Ms. Lois handed Jimmy two slices of cake wrapped in a cloth and she also gave him a basket to carry them in.

"Thank you Ms. Lois," said Jimmy.

"You're welcome young man," replied Ms. Lois.

Ms. Lois waved goodbye to Jimmy and finished hanging clothes. Jimmy was confused at his dreams and wondered what they meant.

He desperately wanted to play music and perhaps even make it as well. That was a discussion for him and the Music Man to have once he returned. "Perhaps I can be his protégé," Jimmy said to himself.

Jimmy arrived at his home, and noticed that nothing had changed. The grass still had snow on it, and the door still needed to be painted.

Jimmy took a deep breath and knocked on the door.

The door opened slowly and his mother just stared at him. Jimmy just stood there, unsure of what to say to her.

Tears fell from his mother's eyes and she said in a very soft but broken voice, "I'm sorry."

She looked down with disappointment, looked back up, and hugged Jimmy.

"I'm so sorry my son."

"I want you to know that I love you very much and I'm very sorry for the things I have said to you."

"Ever since your dad died, it's been very hard for me." "Can you forgive me?"

"Yes mother," Jimmy replied with tears falling from his eyes. "And I love you too."

Jimmy hugged his mother very tightly. "Where were you?" his mother asked. "I'll tell you all about it," smiled Jimmy. "I have some cake for you."

"Can we eat it and talk?" asked Jimmy. "Why of course son." Jimmy explained how he was cold and knocked on a stranger's door.

He talked about how the Music Man let him in and then found out that he too loved music.

He also talked about the dreams that he had and what he wanted to do more than anything.

"I want to play music mother," said Jimmy.

"'May I go back to Mr. Cornelius's house and see which school I can   attend?" "It sounds like it's something you love to do," said his mother. "I did not know," as she looked down again.

A tear fell from her eye. "I'm so sorry Jimmy." "It's okay mother." "We were looking everywhere for you," said his mother.

"The neighbors, police, and I." "I was so scared."

"But you're here now, that's all that matters." His mother looked up and smiled at him. "This cake is delicious," she said as she ate a couple of pieces.

"You should come with me!" exclaimed Jimmy. "You can meet Ms. Lois and Mr. Cornelius." "Okay," laughed his mother.

"I'll get dressed and then you can show me your new friends," she smiled.

Jimmy had not been this happy in a very long time, except in his dreams.

Jimmy and his mother went off to meet Ms. Lois, her boys, and the Music Man.

It was in the afternoon so the sun shone brightly. However, it was still really cold. Also, the snow had pretty much melted, so they only needed wet boots and a jacket.
"I can't believe you walked this far as cold as it was," said Jimmy's mother. "Wasn't really thinking about it," said Jimmy.
"I hurt you that much son?" asked Jimmy's mother.

"It's okay now, I know you're trying really hard," said Jimmy. Jimmy looked up at his mother and she smiled.
"I love you," as she put her arm on his shoulder. "Always remember that."
"Even when you're a famous musician," said Jimmy's mother, as she winked. Jimmy smiled so hard and wide.
"You really think I can become famous?!" asked Jimmy. "Of course," said Jimmy's mother.
"If that's what your heart is telling you to do, then you should do it." Jimmy smiled again and hugged his mom.
"I'm sorry I ran away." "It's okay, I understand," his mother replied. "Now, let's walk faster."

"I'm excited to hear you play!"

Jimmy started to pick up the pace and looked back at his mom. "Okay!"
His boots splashed the wet snow underneath.

"This is Ms. Lois's house," said Jimmy.
"Well let's knock on the door," laughed his mother.

Jimmy knocked on the door and Ms. Lois greeted them with open arms. "Why who is this beautiful young woman?" asked Ms. Lois. "Nice to meet you, I'm Jimmy's mother." "Julia."
"Julia Jakes."

"You have an immaculate home."

Ms. Jakes was blown away by how neat Ms. Lois's home was. Everything was in its place.
"Thank you dear."

"And you have a pretty name," said Ms. Lois. "I'm Lois Weddingfield."
"Nice to meet you Lois," said Ms. Jakes.

"You have a very talented and bright son," said Ms. Lois. "Why thank you," Ms. Jakes said, as she looked at Jimmy.

"Boys!"

"Come meet Jimmy's mother!"

Michael and Morris came running from the kitchen, "Hi there ma'am, I'm Michael."
"I'm Morris!"

"Want something to eat?" "Mother just made stew!"
"Sure, why not?" smiled Ms. Jakes.

Ms. Jakes and Jimmy followed the boys to the kitchen and savored the meal that was before them.
"This is absolutely delicious," said Ms. Jakes. "I helped her!" shouted Morris.
Michael elbowed Morris in the chest. "You only helped her season it."
"I still helped her," sneered Morris.

"I have to learn how to cook," Morris continued to say.

"We'll be moving to the city soon." "Going to try to find work as a builder."
"Put those muscles to use," laughed Ms. Lois. "Find a wife and have children," she added.

"I want to travel, thinking about becoming a sailor," said Michael. "Work and save enough money to get my own boat or ship."
"Well I'm sure your mother has raised you both very well," smiled Ms. Jakes. Ms. Lois looked up and smiled at the compliment Jimmy's mother gave her. "Dessert's next," said Ms. Lois, as she winked at Jimmy.
"This time I made homemade cookies."

"Mr. Cornelius can't stop eating those either." Ms. Lois and Ms. Jakes both laughed.

"I can't wait to meet him," said Ms. Jakes, as she smiled. "Jimmy hasn't been this happy in a long time."

"Neither have I."

"Yes, you'd be amazed at what music can do," said Ms. Lois, as she handed everyone a piece of one of her famous cookies. "Mmm."

"These are delicious," said Ms. Jakes.

"Thank you for inviting us into your home and being kind to my son," said Jimmy's mother as they were saying goodbye. "You're very welcome."

"You're both welcomed here anytime," smiled Ms. Lois.

Jimmy and his mother made their way directly to the Music Man's house.

It was freezing cold, with the snow blowing around them. "Well, this is it mom," said Jimmy.
Julia Jakes was so excited to meet the Music Man.

She knocked on the door and the Music Man opened it. "Hello."
"You must be Jimmy's mother." "My, you're really beautiful."
"Thank you."
"I'm Julia Jakes," as she shook the Music Man's hand. "I'm Cornelius."

"It's so nice to meet you," said Ms. Jakes.

"It's nice to meet you as well," said the Music Man. "You all must be freezing."
"Come, I just made a fresh pot of tea." "The fireplace is nice and toasty too."
"You can sit there," the Music Man said to Jimmy's mother, as he pointed at his sofa chair.
"Would you like a blanket?" he asked.

"No thank you, I think the fire is doing the trick," Ms. Jakes replied.
"Isn't his home peaceful mother?" Jimmy asked.
"Indeed it is," replied Ms. Jakes, as she looked around.

"Would you like a tour?" asked the Music Man, as he handed Jimmy and Ms. Jakes a cup of warm tea.
"I sure would," Ms. Jakes responded.

"What a beautiful piano," she said, as she stood up and observed the beautiful object. "Jimmy."
"You know how to play this son?" "Yes," said Jimmy, in a confident manner.
"Mr. Cornelius has been teaching me the basics, but I mostly can play by ear." "Let's hear it," Jimmy's mother said in an excited manner.
"You want to go to music school right?" "Practice makes perfect." Jimmy was so happy that his mother approved of his abilities and passion. He immediately sat down at the piano bench and started to play.

Jimmy's mother couldn't believe what she was hearing. He played so gracefully, and with much ease.

"I didn't know you could play so well." Jimmy looked back at his mother and smiled.

"Want to see the rest of the house?" asked the Music Man.

"Sure," said Ms. Jakes.

The Music Man showed Jimmy's mother every part of his home, even the attic. She thought to herself how he could live by himself for so long.

"This is where it all started," said the Music Man, as he showed her the attic. "Where WHAT all started?" asked Ms. Jakes. "Jimmy's love for music."

"He fell in love with the piano at first sight."

Jimmy stood outside but decided to listen through the attic door.

"Did he tell you about his dreams?" the Music Man asked.

"Yes," answered Ms. Jakes. She sighed deeply.

"Surely this will only be a hobby for him." "We have to live in reality."

"And in reality, one can not earn a lot of money playing musical instruments." "When Jimmy's father died, I had to earn money as best as I could."

"I work pretty much all day and night."

"He has enough trouble keeping up with his chores." "Jimmy is now very self-sufficient."

"But I don't want this fascination with music to get to his head."

"He's a very bright boy."

"Talented as well," interjected the Music Man.

"Yes, but we barely have enough money to put food on the table."
"I can't afford to pay for him to go to music school."
"So, he can come over here and play once a week if he keeps up with his chores." "Maybe one day, when he's a young man, he can go after this dream of his."
"But not right now."
   Suddenly, Ms. Jakes heard a sniffle.
   She opened the door and found Jimmy crying. "Oh son," cried Ms. Jakes.
Jimmy turned around and ran down the attic stairs and locked himself in the spare room.
"See," Ms. Jakes said as she turned to the Music Man. "This is what happens."
"People have these big dreams and then left only disappointed."
"He has to understand that we are not well-off."
"We are not rich."

"He may even have to get a job soon."

"It's very hard for me, and I'm only getting older."

"I will pay for his classes," said the Music Man in a stern voice.
Ms. Jakes looked up with a shocked look on her face.
"But promise me one thing."

"You will never discourage him from his dream." "When he first knocked on my door, he was very sad." "I was lonely."
"My wife and child died years ago."

"But when Jimmy heard me hum melodies, I could see the love for music in his eyes."
"So, he will play and learn music." "It's what makes him happy."
"Don't worry about the expenses." "He can also live at the school." "It's a boarding music school."
Ms. Jakes looked up with tears streaming down her eyes. "But how?" Ms. Jakes whispered.
"I am very wealthy; I just live very modestly," the Music Man explained. "I don't need much."
"My family is very wealthy."

"But I'm the only one left around these parts."

"I was once a student at the school." "It's where my wife and I met."
"That piano was given to me from my professor." "He was quite famous."
"So don't worry, it will be taken care of." "I may even try to teach at the school."
Ms. Jakes couldn't stop crying, and was left speechless.

She smiled at the Music Man, turned around, and slowly walked down the attic stairs.
"Jimmy," Ms. Jakes said in a quiet voice, as she knocked on the bedroom door. Jimmy sat on the edge of the bed and remained silent, staring at the wall.

"I'm sorry love."

"I believe you are very talented and have a gift, but"

"I also know that you have to have money to go after your dreams in this world." Ms. Jakes sighed and took a deep breath.
"Mr. Cornelius has offered to pay for you to go to the boarding music school to play music."
"Those dreams you had, they meant something to you." "And I know you'll go far."

Suddenly, the door flew open and Jimmy hugged his mother, almost making her lose balance.
"I love you son."

"I just want what's best for you."

Jimmy smiled and kissed her on the cheek.

Jimmy looked up and the Music Man stood in the hallway, smiling at the occasion. Out of nowhere, Jimmy felt very sad.
He remembered Soriya, Phillip, Angela, and Chris.

He smiled however, at the idea that he had the dream, and that he was now happy. "I'm going to go tell Michael, Morris, and Ms. Lois!" Jimmy shouted as he started to run out of the door.
"Jimmy, your coat and boots," said Ms. Jakes. "Thanks mother," said Jimmy, with a wide smile. "We'll go there together," said the Music Man. "They'll be ecstatic."

"What does that mean?" asked Jimmy.

"They'll be very happy for you," said Jimmy's mother.

"Oh, I forgot to mention to you Jimmy," said the Music Man. "I will try to teach at the school."
Jimmy jumped up and down with much excitement. "This is the happiest day of my life!"
The Music Man smiled, laughed, and put on his coat. "Well, it's getting dark."
"Better head over there now."

The Music Man, Ms. Jakes, and Jimmy headed off to share the good news.

Chapter 30

March 12, 1930

"Wow, this school is enormous!"

"We get to make music here?!" shouted Jimmy. "I'm delighted to say yes."
"You're wasting time now my boy," said the Music Man as he laughed. "I'll be in there shortly," he added as he looked at a nearby graveyard. "Wife and son are buried there, just want to say hello."
Jimmy didn't know what to say and decided that silence was the best answer. However, he did want to let the Music Man know that he appreciated everything he did for him.

Jimmy was young but very mature for his age.

"Sir?"

"Yes my boy?" asked the Music Man. "Thank you."
"No."

"Thank you," said the Music Man as he smiled at Jimmy. Jimmy smiled back and opened the door to the music school. He pulled out a map, which indicated where to go.
He felt a sense of being in the school before, but ignored the feeling, hurried and found his classroom.
He walked in slowly.

"Now now, I need to call everyone's name for attendance purposes," said a shorter lady standing at the podium.
She had brown skin, and long black hair. "Hi there," the lady said to Jimmy. "Please, sit anywhere."
"We are just getting started."

Jimmy sat down in an empty chair and looked straight ahead.
Then, a girl leaned into him, and whispered,
"Hi, I'm Soriya."

"Nice clothes," she said with a smile.

"I'm Angela."

"Ahhhhhhh, I am sooooo tired."
"I'm Chris! As he extended his hand, Not many boys in here."

"I'm Phillip."

"This is my first year." "Music is wonderful isn't it?"

Jimmy looked at them, unable to speak. All four were sitting right next to him. "Huh? We've met...," Jimmy started to say, as his face looked with shock.

Then, the lady at the podium said loudly,

"Class, when I call your names, please say here."

Before she could call roll, she looked to the right and said, "Oh, hello there."

"You must be the assistant teacher." "Was just about to call roll."

"You can introduce yourself once I complete roll."

"In the meantime, you can look at the music sheets. They're over there, on the piano."

The Music Man then walked over to the piano and waved hello to the students. He sat down, took a deep breath, and then looked at the music in front of him.

Backstory for the Music Man

Cornelius Waters entered the halls of The Windsart Boarding school. It wasn't a regular boarding school. This boarding school was a music boarding school.

Cornelius could play musical instruments by ear and his father knew that his son was very talented. He managed to get good grades. So, Cornelius's father allowed his son to explore his talent at the boarding school.

Cornelius's father was a wealthy Black man. He was a businessman and was very good at what he did. They owned a mansion and Cornelius didn't want for nothing.

Every chance Cornelius had, he would play music. The first musical instrument Cornelius played, was the piano. His parents bought one for a party they were having. His father didn't know how to play so he hired a pianist to play for guests, at the party. The evening of the party, as everything was being set up, the pianist sat at the piano. His name was Waddell Langston, and he was very easy going. He was rather tall and had to hunch over a little to play successfully.

Cornelius was just five years old when he saw the lovely instrument in the center of the large room.

His nanny must not have been watching him, because the young boy stood in the hallway, staring as the pianist played a piece of music.

"Well, hello there."

"You're a handsome little fellow."

"Would you like to play it with me?" asked Waddell, the pianist.

Cornelius shook his head yes and ran to the piano. He studied the white and black piano keys with keen curiosity.

"Son, get down from there!" shouted Cornelius's mother. She was medium height, with a very elegant look to her.

Her hair was pinned up into a bun, and her makeup wasn't too heavy.

"It's okay Miss," said the pianist, as he placed Cornelius's hand on the piano keys. "What's the fuss?" asked Cornelius's father. Cornelius's father was always busy, always in a hurry.

"Nothing."

"Cornelius just shouldn't be up there." "I'm afraid he's going to break it." "Break what?"

"The piano dear," Cornelius's mother said as she pointed at the piano. "Ah, he'll be fine," said Cornelius's father.

"He's a kid, he's curious."

The pianist started to play his piece and what happened next startled Cornelius's parents.

"My my," said Cornelius's mother, as she placed her hand on her lips.

"I think we have a very talented child dear," said Cornelius's father, as he kissed his wife's cheek.

The pianist overheard Cornelius's parents' remarks and smiled with satisfaction. "Keep it up," said the pianist, as he looked down at Cornelius.

Cornelius had natural talent and played the piano with much ease.

Realizing that he couldn't read music, Cornelius's mother walked up to the piano. "What are you playing dear?"

"Where did you learn that from?"

"It's in my head," replied Cornelius.

Ever since, Cornelius could not stop playing instruments. He played the piano, the violin, and many more instruments. He could even sing.

The boarding school was a four-year program that taught students how to play instruments and make music.

If one was already talented, the school ensured that their craft would be perfected. The professors that taught at the school were world- renowned pianists, violinists, composers, and loved to share their knowledge of music.

Music was always playing in Cornelius's head and now, being at the boarding school, the possibilities were endless.

Thank You

I hope you enjoyed my first novel. You can purchase the remaining books of the Music Man series on my website at MoonyaniWrite.com or on Amazon. The second book of the series is titled, The Music Man: Other Dimensions and the third book is titled, The Music Man: Hidden Portals.

Also, reviews are very important for Authors and they help our books get noticed.
If you could please leave an honest review on my Amazon page or on Goodreads, it would be greatly appreciated.

Thank you so much.

Also, you can follow me on Twitter and Instagram @MoonyaniWrite

Made in the USA
Monee, IL
22 April 2023